THIS YEAR IT
WILL BE DIFFERENT

Also by Maeve Binchy

Light a Penny Candle
Echoes
London Transports
Dublin 4
The Lilac Bus
Firefly Summer
Silver Wedding
Circle of Friends
The Copper Beech
The Glass Lake
Evening Class
Tara Road
Scarlet Feather
Quentins
Nights of Rain and Stars
Whitethorn Woods

Aches & Pains (non-fiction)

THIS YEAR
IT WILL
BE DIFFERENT

Maeve Binchy

This edition first published in Great Britain in 2007
by Orion Books
an imprint of the Orion Publishing Group Ltd
Orion House, 5 Upper St Martin's Lane,
London, WC2H 9EA
An Hachette Livre UK company

1 3 5 7 9 10 8 6 4 2

A CIP catalogue record for this book
is available from the British Library.

ISBN 978 0 7528 7628 3 hardback
ISBN 978 0 7528 9081 4 trade paperback

Typeset by Deltatype Ltd, Birkenhead, Merseyside
Printed in Great Britain by Clays Ltd, St Ives plc

The Orion Publishing Group's policy is to use papers that
are natural, renewable and recyclable products and
made from wood grown in sustainable forests. The logging
and manufacturing processes are expected to conform to
the environmental regulations of the country of origin.

www.orionbooks.co.uk

To dearest Gordon with all my love and thanks

CONTENTS

THIS YEAR IT
WILL BE DIFFERENT

The First Step
of Christmas

Jenny and David gave wonderful Christmas parties. Always on the Sunday before. They asked the whole family, his and hers, they produced Timmy for just enough time for everyone to think he was adorable and never for that one moment too long when people would tire of him. They made the party a huge buffet so that nobody was too trapped with anyone else. The house was festooned with decorations, usually real holly and real ivy gathered from the countryside where it was growing wild. There was nothing vulgar about their tree. Clever ribbons and angels and paper flowers, not expensive-looking packages. But everyone *knew* that somewhere, discreetly, were the gift-wrapped presents that must have poured in to a couple so loving and considerate as David and Jenny.

As the years passed, five Christmases to be precise, Jenny stood sometimes in her immaculate kitchen listening to the murmurs of appreciation. David's first wife had never done anything like this. Oh, no one had been invited across the door in Diana's day. Diana had been far too hoity-toity to bother with family.

That was Jenny's reward. That was the glory for the weeks,

no, months, of preparation and planning and shopping and making it all seem so effortless. David had grumbled slightly when Jenny said they should have a second freezer, but then he wasn't there when she made the mountains of mince pies and the stacks of savouries. David didn't know how Jenny worked in that kitchen on the nights he had meetings or had to stay out of town. He would never know. She would be as different from the beautiful, selfish Diana as it was possible to be. And her child Timmy would be an angel, not a devil, as Diana's child had turned out. Not a dangerous, destructive girl like Alison.

Alison had been nine when Jenny met her first. Very beautiful, with untamed curly hair almost covering her face. She had made no pretence at politeness.

'How much did that cost?' she had asked Jenny about the new dress.

'Why do you want to know?' Jenny was spirited from the very start.

'I was asked to find out.' Alison shrugged as if it didn't matter very much.

'By your mother?' Jenny could have bitten out her tongue the moment she said it.

'Heavens no, Mother wouldn't be remotely interested.' The way she said it, Jenny knew she was speaking the truth; the lovely, lazy Diana would not indeed have cared.

'Who then?'

'The girls at school. One of my friends said you must be after Father for his money.'

It hadn't really got any better.

When she was ten, Alison had come to stay for a weekend and had tried on all Jenny's clothes and used all her make-up. It wouldn't have mattered so much if every single lipstick had not been twisted out of shape, and every garment marked with make-up.

'She was only dressing up, all little girls like doing that,' David said, his eyes pleading.

Jenny decided not to have their first row on the losing battle-field of the stepchild. She managed to smile and planned a lengthy session at the dry cleaners. When Alison was eleven, Timmy was born. 'Did you forget to take your pills?' she asked Jenny when her father was out of the room.

'We wanted him, Alison, just as your mother and father wanted you.'

'Oh yeah?' Alison had said, and Jenny's heart was leaden. It was true that she had wanted the child much more than David had. How could this monstrous stepdaughter have found her vulnerability?

When Alison was twelve, she was expelled from school. The counsellor said that it was all to do with feeling her father had rejected her. She must be allowed to spend more time as part of his life. David was out at work all day, and so was Jenny; they treasured the time they took together with Timmy. Time when the quiet Swiss au pair went to her room and left them to be a family. Now they had Alison on long visits sulking, yawning, contributing nothing, criticising everything.

When she was thirteen, she didn't want to come near them, which was bliss, except that it made David feel rejected. Jenny worked in a publishing house. She told colleagues ruefully that she could see why there were so many books on step-parenting, she had read them all and she could have written half a dozen more. But none of them had ever had to face anything like Alison.

When Alison was fourteen, her mother died. Suddenly and

unexpectedly, after a routine operation. David had gone to Alison's boarding school. 'I expect you'll have to have me now,' she had said to her father. David said it had nearly broken his heart to think that his only daughter considered herself a package to be passed from one place to another. Jenny forced herself to think about Diana, dead before she was forty. Dead without ever having lived properly. She put the thought of Alison to the furthest part of her brain. She knew it would spoil everything. There were going to be no happy endings in this story, no one would walk hand in hand into the sunset swearing undying friendship. She would do it, she would do it for David and, oddly, for the dead Diana, whom she had feared and mistrusted in life. If Jenny were to die young, she would like some other woman to look after Timmy, to try to make a life for him.

She slaved as never before over their Christmas party. Sometimes she got up ludicrously early in the morning. David would come down to breakfast and find a smell of cooking in the kitchen, even though all the mess had been cleared away.

'You are a funny little thing,' he said to her, giving her a squeeze.

Jenny was not funny, nor was she a little thing. She would look at herself thoughtfully. She was tall, not as willowy as Diana, but tall. She was deadly serious about her family and her work. Why was it the action of a funny little thing to get the party right? He used to tell her how much he loved it, that he had always been one for ceremony and for celebration, but Diana had never wanted to bother. But Jenny would pick no fights, manufacture no rows. Not at the festive season.

Alison arrived a day earlier than she was expected. Jenny came back from work and found her halfway through eating a tray of intensely complicated hors d'oeuvres. Each one had taken three minutes to assemble, they would take one second to eat, and Jenny had made sixty of them, shaping the curls of filo pastry with endless patience, and leaving them to cool before freezing them. It represented three hours of her life. She looked at Alison with pure hatred.

Alison looked up from behind the curtain of hair.

'These aren't bad. I didn't know you were a homemaker as well as a career woman.'

Jenny's face was white with rage.

Even Alison noticed.

'These weren't for supper or anything, were they?' she said with mock contrition.

Jenny took the deep breath that all the books on step-parenting seemed to recommend. It was so deep, it reached her toes.

'Welcome home, Alison,' she said. 'No, these weren't for supper ... not at all. They were just something for the party.'

'Party?'

'Yes, on Sunday. We have the family. It's a tradition.'

'I think things have to be more than just three or four years to be a tradition,' Alison said.

'This is our sixth Christmas together, so I suppose that feels like a tradition.' Jenny's shoes were hurting, she wanted to take one of them off and beat her stepdaughter senseless with its high sharp heel. But she felt it would have been both unseasonal and counter-productive. There was no way Jenny was going to enjoy this Christmas; what she must try to do was to contain it. She tried to remember that phrase people used – what was it? damage limitation? – she had never known quite what it meant. Had it something to do with saving what you could? She often found at work that if you thought of something quite irrelevant and allowed your mind to click through the motions, then it prevented you from flying off the handle.

She saw Alison looking at her with interest.

'Yeah, I suppose six years is a tradition,' Alison agreed, as if she were struggling to be fair.

A glow of sympathy towards the girl began to shine through the mists of dislike and resentment. But Jenny was too experienced to mistake it for the swell of violins surging at the end of the movie.

'About the party,' Jenny said. 'Are there any of your mother's relations that we might ask?'

Alison looked at her in disbelief. 'Ask here?'

'Yes, it's your home now, they are your relations, too. We want to make it a family Christmas, we would be very happy to have them.'

'What for?'

'For the same reason that anyone asks anyone under their roof at Christmas, for goodwill, for friendship.' Jenny hoped her voice wasn't getting tinny, she could feel the edge developing.

She willed her eyes away from the tray of canapés that she had worked on so meticulously. The crumby, mangled remains. Even those that had not been eaten were somehow used-looking.

'That's not why people have Christmas parties, it's for showing off,' Alison said.

Jenny took off her shoes and sat down at the table. She reached out for the perfectly formed pastries with their exquisite fillings. They tasted very good.

'Is that what you think?' she asked Alison.

'I don't think it. I know it.'

Jenny did a calculation in her head: fourteen now, Alison

might be with them until she was eighteen. With any luck, this school might not expel her, so it was only the school holidays and half terms they had to consider, four Easters, four summers, four Christmases. Timmy would grow up in the shadow of this moody girl. He would be a grown-up seven-year-old by the time Alison left their home. She would lose these lovely years because of the hostile girl who sat at her kitchen table. She wondered what she would do if it were a problem at work. But that was not a useful road to go down. If Alison had been a mulish, mutinous junior, she would have been sacked or transferred with such speed that it would have electrified everyone. She contemplated telling this discontented girl that life, far from being a bowl of cherries, could often be a bed of nettles and that everyone had to make her own happiness. But Jenny was familiar enough with teenagers to know that they wouldn't share that kind of pain as an older woman might. Someone of Alison's age would shrug and ask, Why bother?

She wondered, was there a chance that Alison might be into the bond of the friendship? Should she offer to exchange some of her blood with her and swear eternal solidarity?

But sadly, she remembered the school reports. They had all stressed how much Alison resented any of the school conventions, even those enjoyed by her peers. No, the sisterly loyalty act didn't look as if it would work.

She ate her fifth canapé, thinking that this now represented a quarter of an hour's work early that morning. Soon David would be home, tired and anxious to have a restful evening. She hadn't even seen her beloved Timmy since she came in the door.

All over the country, families were getting ready for Christmas, some of them certainly had tensions … but not one family, in the entire land, had Alison. The time bomb. Theirs for four long years, ready to explode at any time.

She saw Alison's luggage strewn all around the place. She would *have* to get an agreement with David that Alison keep everything in her room. Her room! Nothing had been done to it.

In fact, it was filled with boxes; worse still, packets of fir cones and a huge canvas bag of holly sprigs. If ever the child was going to feel unwanted and unwelcome, it would be because of Jenny. She had intended to leave many, many clothes hangers and a small understated vase with greenery and a couple of flowers as welcome ... nothing that could be considered showy or vulgar or uncool, or whatever were the favourite hatreds of Alison this festive season.

She had been silent as she had been glumly rejecting every possible method of relating to her stepdaughter. Alison must have noticed the lack of chatter. Her eyes followed Jenny's and landed on the luggage.

'I suppose you want me to take all that out of your way,' Alison said in the voice of a martyr who had met a particularly unpleasant torturer.

'About your room ...' Jenny began.

'I'll keep the door closed,' Alison groaned.

'No, not that ...'

'*And* I'll keep the music down,' she said, rolling her eyes.

'Alison, it's the room I wanted to explain ...'

The girl stopped in her bag-laden trudge to the bedroom.

'Oh God, Jenny, what is it *now*? What else can't I do?'

Jenny felt so tired, she could cry.

'I just wanted to explain what there was in there ...' she said in a weak voice. Alison had opened the door.

She stood looking around her at all the preparations, the trimmings and the garnish for a festive Christmas. She lifted a fir cone and smelled it. Her eyes went all around the room as if she couldn't take it all in. 'We didn't think you were coming until tomorrow,' Jenny apologised.

'You were going to decorate my room.' Alison's voice was husky.

'Well, yes. Well, with whatever you thought ... you know.' Jenny sounded confused.

'With all this?' Alison looked around her.

Jenny bit her lip. There was enough greenery in that room to decorate a three-storey house, which was what they lived in. The child couldn't possibly have thought it was all for her bedroom.

Then with one look at Alison's radiant face she realised that that was exactly what the tall, rangy Pre-Raphaelite with the wild hair and the sullen mouth was. She was a child. A motherless child who was going to have a room decorated for the first time.

In publishing they always told you that the best decisions, the best books, came by accident, not by dint of long and clever planning.

'Yes, well, with most of it. I thought we'd make it look really nice, nice and welcoming for you. But now that you're here ... maybe ...'

'Maybe I could help?' Alison said with eyes shining.

It wouldn't last for ever, Jenny knew that. The road ahead was not lit with soft, flattering lighting like a movie. They wouldn't fall into each other's arms. But it would last a little bit. Maybe through the party and through Christmas Day.

She heard the sound of her son running to find her.

'Where were you, you didn't come and see me?' he called.

She picked him up in her arms. 'I was just welcoming your sister home,' she said, almost afraid to look at Alison's face.

Alison leaned out and tickled Timmy with a frond of ivy. 'Happy Christmas, little brother,' she said.

The Ten Snaps
of Christmas

Maura loved Christmas. Jimmy endured it. When Maura was a child they used to make a great fuss of it, an Advent calendar opening a window each day, the Christmas cards examined with all the verses read aloud, then each one threaded on coloured string. They would start talking about the tree as early as October, and every present was lovingly wrapped and labelled and laid under the tree for at least a week's squeezing and prodding in the hope and even fear of finding out what it was.

When they first got married, Jimmy thought this was very endearing, he used to kiss her on the nose and say she was sweet. As the years went by, Maura noticed that it had become less sweet, like so many things. So she kept her sense of Christmas excitement a secret that she hugged to herself and the babies as they arrived one by one. This year there was only Rebecca for Father Christmas. Rebecca was four, John and James and Orla were far too old. But you couldn't be too old for trees and lights and candles and a holly wreath for the door. Maura worked alone and happily, and didn't burden Jimmy too much when he came home from work in the evenings. She only consulted him about what Big Present each child was to get.

James was ten: he would get a bicycle. John was eight: he would get the electronic game that had been much hinted at. Rebecca would get a dozen small, noisy things – she wasn't old enough for the Big Present yet, but Orla ... what would they give the tall fourteen-year-old? Maura said she thought Orla might like a voucher for clothes in that trendy shop where her school friends spent hours just looking in the window. Jimmy thought that Orla might like a typewriter and a quickie typing course. They could come to no meeting of minds over this at all. Maura said to give anyone a typing course for Christmas was like giving a woman a diet book or a membership to Weight Watchers. Jimmy said to give a child a voucher for a shop like that was like a licence to buy perverted transsexual clothing with a parental imprimatur. It had better be neither of these. They decided they would give her a Polaroid camera. The kind that would take pictures instantly there and then. Festive for the season and urgent for today's generation. So that was what they bought, and wrapped it in many other boxes and corrugated paper so that Orla prodded it a hundred times and still had no idea what it contained until the day itself.

Maura bought some heated hair rollers for her mother, who came to stay for Christmas. Her mother was glamorous and fashion-conscious in Maura's mind; in Jimmy's mind she was mutton dressed as lamb, a woman who refused to grow old gracefully. He never objected to her Christmas visit, but he didn't look forward to it either. His own parents were kept at a safe distance, presents posted and a call on Christmas morning to wish them the compliments of the season. Jimmy's family was a lot less demonstrative.

Maura bought a nice Tara brooch for Marie-France, the French au pair girl. Marie-France had this disconcerting habit of wondering were things real silver or pure silk or was the wine vintage or if they had the best seats at the theatre. At least with something so obviously ethnic and Irish she could hardly complain. Marie-France was all right, Maura thought, a bit pouty and shruggy and eyes-up-to-heavenish, but maybe that was the way twenty-year-old French girls banished to learn English behaved. She did exactly what she was asked to do with Rebecca and about preparing the vegetables and vacuuming the downstairs, but not one single thing more. Maura had often wished she had set out a slightly more demanding timetable; after all, Marie-France had a room of her own, three marvellous meals a day, and endless time to study as well as go to her course. But nothing, not even the minor sense of grudge towards Marie-France, could spoil Maura's Christmas. She felt the familiar excitement just as soon as they started to play 'Mary's Boy Child' and 'The Little Drummer Boy' over the tannoy at the supermarkets ... and that was fairly early on. By the time the streetlights were up, Maura was in a high state of happy fuss. Her mother arrived with a yet more outrageous outfit than usual, her friend Brigid who had left her husband again wondered was it possible if she could join the family, and Maura said, 'Of course,' for Christmas was a time to be happy and Brigid had been a friend since school. Jimmy groaned a bit about Brigid. He said she was a nutcase and that the husband was well rid of her, but he agreed that since she could only eat a plate of turkey and ham, and since the day was ruined already by the presence of Maura's mother, then honestly he saw no objection to Brigid coming, and sure if she brought her sleeping bag why not, why not let her sleep in the sitting room on the sofa. Since the crazy mother-in-law was taking up the guest room why not?

They sang carols on Christmas Eve. Maura closed her eyes in happiness and in gratitude for all she had. Her face was so happy that even Orla who thought it was yucky, and Grannie who thought it was over the top, and Brigid who thought it was barking mad, and Jimmy who thought it was pathetic, all joined in. James and John thought it was funny and sang one louder than the other. Rebecca thought it was a game and banged on her tambourine in what she thought was in time with the music.

Next morning after Mass they sat around in a circle while the presents were given out. Maura's mother loved the hair rollers and took a plug off one of the lamps immediately in order to try them out. Marie-France shrugged and pouted over the Tara brooch, Jimmy was genuinely pleased with the anorak because he hated waste and he wanted one anyway, and Maura showed pleasure at the carpet sweeper, which Jimmy said might be useful on those occasions when she didn't think it worthwhile taking out the vacuum cleaner.

Orla was very quiet all morning as the gifts were being opened. Maura felt a pang of regret. Perhaps she should have fought harder for the voucher for the child. It was becoming harder and harder to talk to her, but all mothers said the same about teenage daughters, and really it was only now when she was well and truly married and had a grown family that she could relate properly to her own mother. Maybe that was one relationship that would never work. It would be the same when chubby, adorable Rebecca had a decade behind her. Orla wasn't rude or surly like other people's daughters. She never defied them or insisted on her own way. It was just that recently she seemed ... well ... a little bored with them. It was as if she didn't rate them very highly as a family. Nothing you could put your finger on and certainly nothing you could say to Jimmy, who thought the sun and the moon and all of the stars shone out of his eldest daughter. It would look like some kind of criticism, which it was not. Maura had decided on this occasion, as on many others, to say nothing. But she chewed her lip as Orla's long blonde hair fell over the well-disguised present and finally revealed the camera that would take instant pictures.

'It's beautiful, thank you, Dad, thank you, Mum,' she said in roughly the same voice that Maura had thanked Jimmy for the carpet sweeper.

'You can get people to take pictures of you so that you can chart your progress from ugly duckling to swan,' said Maura's mother.

'Thank you, Grannie,' said Orla.

'Or you could take pictures of fellows and congratulate your-self later that you had nothing to do with them,' said Brigid, who was sitting smoking, angrily rejoicing in her abandoned husband.

'Yes, terrific idea, Auntie Brigid,' said Orla.

Maura could see the annoyance, but yet she too felt dis-appointed. If only Orla knew what she had been saved from ... a typing course to be taken during the school holidays at Easter and a reconstituted typewriter and a book to practise from. If Orla knew that, maybe she might smile more warmly at her mother. Again Maura wished she had stood out for the gift token. If Orla had that in her hand, maybe the day would have been filled with dreams of gear to be bought, to be discussed, tried on, rejected, taken out on approval. Still it was done now and a camera with a whole film of ten snaps in it was a marvellous gift for a fourteen-year-old girl.

'Will you take one now?' James was anxious to see if it worked.

'We'll all make faces.' John wanted it to be a joke.

'Let me take the rollers out first.' Maura's mother was already testing the strength of her new gift and her head was a forest of spikes.

Orla shrugged. She was developing this very unattractive shrug, Maura thought. Far too like Marie-France, far too distant.

'It's Orla's camera, she can take what she likes,' Maura said, and hoped for a grateful smile, a thank-you look. But Orla just shrugged again.

'It doesn't matter,' she said. 'I'll take one if you want to.'

They spent a long time posing. Marie-France had to put on her lipstick. Maura noticed she didn't bother to put on the Tara brooch. Soon they were assembled, four adults on the sofa, the three children in front. Orla pressed the button and like magic it came out a piece of grey-green that turned in front of their eyes into a picture of them all.

They looked oddly dead, Maura thought, and some of them had devil-like red eyes.

They all said it was very clever and wondered what would savages who had never heard of such things think if they saw one.

They had little jobs for the Christmas lunch; the boys had to clear up all the paper and put it in a neat pile. Jimmy was to get the wine. Grannie was to arrange the crackers on the table and lay out the chocolates on little glass dishes to be served later. Brigid was given a new linen dishcloth to polish the glasses. Marie-France had been given nothing, so nothing was what she would do. Maura went out to do the gravy and the bread sauce. Everything seemed to boil at once, the dishes were heavy, and Rebecca was under her feet at every turn. Sharply she ordered the child out of the kitchen and then felt guilty. It was Christmas Day, why was she being so irritable? She just felt that something was wrong. It was one of those silly fears, like recovering from a bad dream. In her annoyance and confusion she let the turkey slip right off the dish onto the floor. She grabbed it furiously by the legs and rammed it back in the baking tin. Thank God her mother and Jimmy hadn't been in the kitchen, they were both great at wrinkling up the nose and sighing at what were called Maura's slapdash methods. What they don't know won't harm them, she thought as she rescued the sausages from under the cooker and picked off the surface dust. She hadn't noticed Orla in the kitchen, but the child was there still examining the camera thoughtfully.

'Do you really like it, my love?' Maura asked kindly.

'Oh yes, didn't I say I did?' The girl was withdrawn. She would only resist any attempt at a heart-to-heart.

'Did the flash go off just then? I was wondering was I seeing lights in front of my eyes, or was it lightning?'

Orla shrugged. I'm going to get that bloody shrug out of her without having to go as far as physical violence, Maura thought purposefully. The boys came into the kitchen.

'Will you take another? Take one of us outside,' they begged.

'No.'

'Oh go on, Orla, that's what it's for.'

'No, they said I could take what I liked.'

'What *are* you going to take?' They were impatient with her now.

'Just casual pictures here and there; you know, to get a picture of Christmas the way it really is, not all people just posing and smiling.'

They lost interest in her. Maura beamed, however. Perhaps Orla did like the gift and she might even take up an interest in photography. That would be marvellous. Maura didn't praise the idea too much in case Orla might shrug it off.

Orla went to the shed where the wine was kept. Daddy didn't hear her come in and had no idea she was there until the flash and the soft whir announced her.

'*Orla*,' he roared, moving towards her very fast. It was almost like a speeded-up film to see how quickly he had drawn away from Marie-France and how his arms had fallen from her. Marie-France looked at the door with a half smile. She was straightening her blouse.

'What kind of a silly trick is that?' Her father wasn't quick enough. Orla was back in the house and Maura had come out to see what the commotion was.

'Nothing, I'm just taking my own pictures for myself like you said I could.'

'Oh leave her, Jimmy. It's her camera, let her take what she likes.' Maura went back to the kitchen.

'It's just a game, you know, a sort of Christmas game,' Jimmy said, desperate, but Maura had lost interest and Orla had gone off somewhere to examine the picture in peace.

Brigid was in the dining room thoughtfully polishing the glasses for the festive lunch, but her thoughts were in no way pleasant. Why was she being forced to camp out in someone else's house, share another family's Christmas because of that bastard? She would show him. She would certainly punish him for this. If only she had some money. Life was so unfair. Look at all this cut glass and silver in Maura's house, they hardly bothered with it. That little dish on the sideboard might be worth a few pounds, and there it was with pencils and sticky tape in it.

As she slipped it into her handbag Brigid heard a hiss and saw the flash. Orla stood impassive at the door.

'I was just dusting it Orla, you know, rubbing it against something in my bag.'

'I know, Auntie Brigid.' Orla was gone before she could be asked to show the picture.

In the sitting room where Grannie was meant to be sorting sweets and crackers, Grannie was actually drinking the festive brandy from a bottle that she was holding by the neck. She nearly choked when Orla came into the room and her look was wide-eyed when she heard the camera make its whishing sound.

'Don't be a silly child, that's a very babyish thing to do wasting your ten snaps, throwing them away.'

'I know, Grannie, but I *am* very babyish,' said Orla.

It was almost time for lunch, soon there would be excited calls from Maura and everyone would gather. The boys were suspiciously quiet. Orla went to their room and entered without knocking. John was coughing over his cigarette but James was flourishing his in fine style.

'Captured for the future generations,' Orla said as the camera flashed.

'We'll be killed,' James said simply. 'It'll ruin Christmas.'

'Only if they see it,' Orla said.

In her own bedroom as she waited for her mother to call, she laid out her collection. The group on the couch and the floor, scarlet-eyed and sure of themselves. Then her mother and the turkey on the floor, her father and Marie-France, her grannie drinking the brandy from the bottle, her mother's friend stealing the silver, her two brothers smoking in their bedroom. She still had four more to take. Maybe one when the plum pudding came in and one when they were all asleep with their mouths open.

'It's ready.' She could hear her mother's excited voice from below.

She tore the picture of the turkey into tiny pieces. Her mother was kind. Pathetic but kind. Orla's eyes went back to her gallery. And look at the great Christmas that her mother had as a result of being kind. No, there was no need to keep the turkey disaster, but she would keep the rest.

She went down to her Christmas lunch with her head held high. She knew somehow she would be a person of importance this year. A person not to be taken lightly any more.

Miss Martin's Wish

Elsa Martin had never been to New York. She had a passport, even a visa to go to the United States, dating from when she had thought that she was going on her honeymoon in Florida.

That was when she had thought she was going to have a honeymoon.

The passport lay there in a box. It was in the same drawer as her grandmother's little silver bag, and all the good-luck cards in an album that the children had made for Miss Martin. She could have thrown them out, but the children had gone to so much trouble, put so many horseshoes and wedding bells on them, such glitter and decoration. It would have been like breaking up blossoms or standing on seashells.

For a while she had kept Tim's letters there; the letter where he told her he had never really loved her and couldn't go through with it, where he begged her forgiveness. But then after a year Elsa had taken the letter and burned it because often she found herself going to read it over and over again. As if she might find some insight, some reason why he had left; some thread of hope that he might be coming back.

People said that Elsa had been magnificent, they said that Tim must have been a rat or mentally unstable. They said she was well rid of him, and they marvelled that she had taken it so calmly, ten days before her wedding day. She had returned gifts with a courteous and noncommittal note: 'Since by mutual consent our marriage will now not take place we would like to return your generous present with our gratitude for your kind wishes.' And she had continued teaching the following term as if nothing had happened, as if her heart had not broken into two separate pieces.

The children were more honest.

'Are you very sad you didn't get married, Miss Martin?' a child might ask.

'A little sad, not very sad,' she would admit with a smile.

In the staff room they didn't ask about the cancelled wedding, and Elsa didn't want to fill them in, so it remained one of life's mysteries. Probably a mismatch, better they found out before the ceremony, really, than afterwards.

Elsa's sisters had never liked Tim because he had small eyes. They told each other, but did not tell Elsa, that their little sister had had a lucky escape.

Elsa's friends hadn't really got to know Tim very well. They were sympathetic but vaguely relieved. Tim had come out of nowhere very quickly and taken all Elsa's mind and attention. Perhaps it was doomed from the start. And the years went by, five of them. The children grew up and forgot that Miss Martin had ever planned a wedding for which they had all made cards. The other teachers in the school forgot too. If a new teacher came and inquired about Miss Martin's private life, they would have to root around in their memories of the incident some years back. A wedding called off at the last moment? It didn't rate as important in their lives. But it was still the centre of Elsa's life. She tried everything possible to uproot the burning anxiety to know why someone thought she was a fine person to share his life hopes and dreams with one day, and the next day was able to say that it had all been a mistake. If it wasn't anything she had *done*, then it must be something to do with the person she *was*. It was a huge matter to put behind you, but of course you had to pretend to – otherwise people accused you of brooding and tried to take you out of yourself, which was wearying and irritating. Elsa's friends thought she was very absorbed with her school work, her colleagues thought she had a busy life with friends. It was easy to remain within yourself, which was where she wanted to be.

Christmas was always meant to be the poignant time, the season that pointed out what the lonely were lacking; but, oddly, Elsa never found that Christmas was any worse than other times. One year she had gone to one sister's, a tense household in south London where a lot of the discussion centred around alcohol and whether her brother-in-law was possibly partaking of too much of it. Another year to another sister's, a haphazard home where Elsa did most of the cooking and clearing up; and then to a colleague's house where they had rather too much carol singing and rather too little food. Last Christmas she had spent walking in the Scottish Highlands with a recently divorced friend who wanted to talk angrily about the innate badness of men and how they should all be wiped from the face of the earth.

And now it was the fifth Christmas. For some reason this year she refused every offer, always grateful, always assuring them of something else long planned, but never specified. At the Christmas concert in the shabby prefabricated annex that served as a school hall, she adjusted the wings of the angels, the fleece of the shepherds, and the crowns of the Three Wise Men as she had done for so many years in this school. The children were overexcited, surrounded by their admiring and proud parents. They all flocked to Elsa and hugged her good-bye. And as she did so often, Elsa thought that teaching was so much better than any other job, particularly at Christmas. Imagine if you were in an office with interminable Christmas parties. How could anyone bear the false cheer, the fake bonhomie?

'Where are you going for Christmas, Miss Martin?' they asked her from the comfort and safety of their parents' arms.

Usually she said something vague and noncommittal, and that she would try not to eat too much Christmas pudding. But this year for some reason one of the children, little Marion Matthews, said confidently to the others, 'She's going to America. She told us she was.'

Had she? Elsa hadn't remembered saying anything of the sort.

'Remember? Miss Martin's going to make a wish for us from the Statue of Liberty,' cried Marion triumphantly.

Elsa remembered. There had been some story they read in class about people making a wish when they passed the Statue of Liberty in New York.

'Have you made a wish there, Miss Martin?' they had asked.

'No, not yet,' Elsa had said. 'But when I go I'll make a wish for you all.'

They had considered it with the seriousness of seven-year-olds. Would Miss Martin wish for the new hall for them? If they had a new hall, they could do all kinds of things, dancing classes, basketball, proper gymnastics. Elsa had said lightly that of course she would, but they must remember that all wishes didn't necessarily come true.

The Christmas holidays began. The children would have forgotten next term that Miss Martin was going to make a wish for them. Their minds would be too full of the adventures and gifts of a busy holiday. But Elsa didn't forget. She went to the drawer to look for her passport. Her face had looked different then, she thought, the eyes less weary, the mouth more relaxed. But perhaps this was fantasy.

At the back of the passport were ten folded notes, each for twenty dollars. They had been there for five years, losing value. Why had she not changed them back into pounds? Perhaps it had all been too painful at the time, and then she had forgotten them. Still, it was a good omen. A whole two hundred extra dollars to spend on herself when she got there. She would give herself some little luxury. She would think not at all of what the money had been intended for. She didn't even know why it was there. Had she changed it herself, was it a gift? Strange that she could remember so much about that time with frightening clarity and other things not at all.

It was surprisingly easy for a single woman to buy a ticket to New York and ask a travel agency to book her a hotel room. Nobody asked her why she was going there. Elsa was an adult, she presumably had plans of her own, her own *agenda*.

Other passengers read their books, watched the movie, or snoozed on the flight.

'Have a good Christmas, you hear?' the man at Immigration instructed her.

'Enjoy your stay,' ordered the man at Customs.

'Best city in the world,' volunteered the bus driver.

At the hotel the receptionist asked if she'd like a little

Christmas tree in her room or not. 'Some folks do, some folks want to forget the holiday, so we always ask,' she said.

Elsa thought for a moment. 'I'd love a little Christmas tree,' she said. For five years she had not even placed a sprig of holly in her flat at home.

She put on her comfortable shoes – she had already forgotten what time it was back in Britain – and went out to mix with the shoppers and the crowds coming home from work. She had heard that New York was a busy, frightening place, where they pushed past you on the street, but the people seemed courteous to her, and smiled when they heard her accent.

She watched the skaters at Rockefeller Center and marvelled at the fairy lights twinkling on every tree along the huge avenues of Manhattan. She stared, fascinated, into the windows of the great department stores, and the lavish displays of gifts. Exhausted, she returned to her own hotel and the individual tree trimmed in her honour by a little oriental chambermaid.

'Do your family celebrate Christmas?' Elsa asked. Back home she would never have asked a personal question about anyone's background or culture. Perhaps being in New York was changing her personality.

'Everybody love Christmas holidays, people are happy and good-tempered,' said the girl, as if it were the most obvious thing in the world.

At the reception desk they had a brochure advertising a Christmas Eve treat. It was a special tour: it began with children singing carols, then it took you around New York in a big bus pointing out the sights and the way various communities celebrated Christmas. There was a festive lunch and then a boat trip to blow away the cobwebs. They would go past the Statue of Liberty.

'Do people make a wish there or is that in my imagination?' Elsa asked.

'I don't know that they do, but then I was born and raised here so I wouldn't know. Perhaps all visitors or first-time people seeing the statue make a wish,' answered the receptionist.

Elsa studied the tour again. It was certainly full of interest, but it was expensive. Then she remembered her magic money, the ten twenty-dollar bills she had not known were hers. 'I'll book it,' she said.

There were twenty of them setting out. Couples and people on their own. They each wore a paper name badge as big as a dinner plate. 'Merry Christmas – I'm Elsa.' Some of them photographed each other.

'Shall I take one of you with your camera?' a man asked Elsa. She didn't like to tell him that there was nobody on the face of the earth to whom she would show such a picture, but he looked kind.

'I'd love that,' she said, not to disappoint him.

They got to know about each other, the people on the tour: the Vietnamese couple whose son had been killed in the war more than thirty years ago. They had corresponded over the years with an American couple whose son had been killed on the same day. This was their first visit. Elsa looked at the four old people in their seventies sitting together in such solidarity and mystification at what had happened to them all those years ago. It made her own problems seem small.

There were a mother and daughter who fought good-naturedly and almost automatically as they had done for a generation and would do for another. There was a scattering of people on their own, all extroverts, all able to talk as if they were old friends. The only quiet person was the man with the kind face who had taken Elsa's photograph for her. He smiled as they passed places by. He looked as if he knew New York well, and might even be from the city, but that would be odd. Why would a native New Yorker take a guided tour of his own place?

Light snow began to fall as they approached the Statue of Liberty. Elsa looked at it with awe. You *must* be able to make a wish at a place like this, a symbol so important to so many people who had come to start a new life with hearts full of hope. She closed her eyes and wished that the children in her school would get a new hall.

'It's not a very important thing,' she said, struggling to be fair, mouthing the words without realising it. 'There must have been more important wishes made here, but I did promise the children I'd ask. And it would make a difference to music and concerts and everything as well as games. It's not just for showing off, and there aren't any funds left to build one, you see.'

She felt a camera flash; the man with the kind face had taken a picture of her.

'You were praying so hard I wanted to record it for you,' he said. He was easy to talk to. She told him about the hall and the schoolchildren back in London, and later when they were having eggnog in a tavern with the group she told him about Tim and how he had left her and about the dollars in the back of her passport.

And he told her about his friend Stefan, who had died six months ago. How every year on Christmas Eve, Stefan had come out to thank the Statue of Liberty for giving him a home in America, but that he had never been able to give Stefan a real home because his father was old and his mother frail, and they could not take on board their only son having a friendship with a man. They still lived in hope that he would marry and that all their great wealth could be handed on to future generations.

He had never been able to spend Christmas Day with Stefan; for years he had sat, mute and miserable, trying to be cheerful for two elderly people who were disappointed in him, trying to put out of his mind the thought of Stefan sitting lonely and confused in an apartment drinking a bottle of vodka but assuring himself that he was loved even though it couldn't be acknowledged.

So every Christmas Eve they had been together and come out to salute the Statue of Liberty at the gate of New York's harbour. And sometimes Stefan played the violin to say thank you for being invited into America. People had smiled at him, some had thought it sentimental, some had thought it touching.

He had tears in his eyes as he spoke of Stefan and how he had promised him that one day he would build a great auditorium in his name so that everyone would know of him. He wouldn't be one more immigrant, he would be a violinist who loved this city. But he couldn't do it yet. Not yet while his parents were alive. He must allow them peace in their last years, months even. Stefan would understand.

'Did he play in concerts?' Elsa asked.

'No, he taught music in a school,' said the man with the kind face, and then suddenly they both knew how Stefan's monument could be built and where. A hall with his name on it could go up three thousand miles away. The children would be pleased but not astonished. Miss Martin had made a wish, that was all. And Stefan could be honoured in another great city until the time was right for him to be acknowledged in New York, his own hometown.

How About You?

Mainly Ellie liked them. The old people who had come to live and often to die in Woodlawns, the hotel for retired folk. There were gardens to walk in, a riverbank to explore and a few nice old trees. Not *exactly* a wood, but still it was as good a name as any other and better than some. The place down the road was called Rest Haven and the one further on was Santa Rosa della Marina. Woodlawns had a little more dignity somehow.

Ellie was popular with the guests. She didn't call them dear or dearie like some of the carers did. She didn't speak to them as if they were deaf or mad. She never asked how are *we* feeling today. She didn't lower her voice in respect of their huge age and imminent death. Ellie would admit to them when she had a hangover or tell them tales about her difficult boyfriend. Eager, untidy and loud, she brought life and energy into their bedrooms with their early-morning tea, and into the Day Room with their mid-morning coffee. Her hair was all over the place, because she was always running to be somewhere that she was needed. She spent little time in the staff room preening herself at a mirror. Ellie prattled on to the guests, asking about their families, she had a natural kindness that more than made up for a sloppy, careless and overfamiliar style of going on. She remembered the names of the visitors, too, which was a bonus, and she had a tendency to flirt with some of the sons or grandsons who came to visit the elderly.

Ellie had only been working at Woodlawns for a short while. She was between jobs and her love life was not working out at all as well as it should have been. Yet again there were problems with Dan. He had definitely promised that they would be together for a Christmas holiday and now he was saying it had only been a vague arrangement.

Ellie had spent all her money on clothes for the trip. Now she was flat broke. She had hoped that Dan would ask her to move in with him, but he hadn't so she also needed somewhere to stay. She would be as good as gold, she had promised. Kate could rely on her.

Kate very much doubted it. She looked at her younger sister, Ellie. Eager and lively, yes. Trusting and enthusiastic, yes. But reliable? No.

And she had no sense about men. This latest one, Dan, had been no great addition to the scene. Several times he had driven in late at night, hooting his horn just when the residents were going to sleep. Ellie was selling herself short by staying with him. That wasn't the way to treat men. Ellie was a good-looking woman, she didn't have to beg like this.

But then Kate was no real example of how a woman should treat a man.

Her own husband had disappeared with a woman much younger than Kate, and somehow without leaving her half of their property. It had not been properly sorted out and never would be. There were still huge debts hanging over Woodlawns. They would need at least five more residents if the place was going to pay for itself.

But of course Donald, Georgia, Hazel and Heather – the very unpleasant hard core of Woodlawns – weren't making things any easier for anyone. They made life a misery for everyone who came into the place, and staff had left because of them. They alienated newcomers with their complaints about Woodlawns. She would love to have said goodbye to them all, but she couldn't.

They literally had nowhere else to go, no family, no friends and no other horizons. They would stay for Christmas when all the others went out. They were particularly trying at Christmas.

Donald would talk about the crime statistics and how different things had been when *he* was a judge. Georgia would say that no one had any class or style these days, unlike in her youth when she was a successful actress, when people *really* knew how to live.

Hazel and Heather would bicker about the old days when Mummy and Daddy were alive and there were proper standards. It was so sad, when you came to think of it. Four people who could have got something out of life but were prepared to give nothing in return. They would stay in Woodlawns, complaining and resentful while the twenty other inhabitants would go to relatives and friends. Twenty *normal* people, who had friends or some kind of family ready to receive them. People who would ask Kate to help them order wine or chocolates to take with them as a gift. People who would return with photographs of jolly Christmas Day lunches where the guests wore paper hats.

But not the hard core.

These four would sit, backs rigid with disapproval, waiting for food to be served, food which would be much criticised.

Donald and Georgia would sit at their individual tables. The sisters, Heather and Hazel, would sit together whispering and commenting. It was not the ideal Christmas, Kate sighed to herself. But at least this year she would probably have Ellie to help her. And when the four had retired for the night, maybe they could have a drink together. Normally she managed it all on her own, not daring to ask any of her staff to share the horrors of the monstrous Georgia, Donald, Heather and Hazel at their very worst. But then Kate knew that Ellie might well disappear if the lout Dan crooked his little finger.

She reminded herself that she was only Ellie's big sister, not her mother. Their mother had given up on both of them. She lived on the other side of the country, tut-tutting whenever either of her daughters was mentioned. So Kate was totally unprepared for the phone call that brought the news of her mother's stroke. It came a few days before Christmas, as the guests and staff were beginning the long, slow business of winding down operations. The stroke was not considered life-threatening but one of them should be there. It had better be Kate – Mother and Ellie were more volatile together. So this meant she would have to close Woodlawns.

Kate sighed a heavy sigh. At least it put the shock and flood of racing emotions about her mother onto one side. What would she do with them all? She might get Donald into Rest Haven. She *might*. But then he was so choleric and bad-tempered and he waved his stick so imperiously ... Yet Rest Haven had pretensions about snobbery and class. Donald was the most top-drawer of the hard core. She wondered which was going to be harder, persuading Rest Haven or persuading Donald.

And then Georgia? She had been banned from Rest Haven over some drinking incident, and from Santa Rosa della Marina because she said that Spanish and Italians made excellent maids but one shouldn't have to talk to them socially.

Hazel and Heather might be easier. They weren't actually *old*, they were just dysfunctional. If she could slide them in before Rest Haven or Santa Rosa actually realised how filled with hate they were … ?

She sat for a while with her head in her hands.

Ellie came in. 'Hangover?' she asked sympathetically.

'Sit down, Ellie.' Kate told her sister the facts briskly and unsentimentally. No, mother wasn't going to die but she would be limited in what she could do. Kate must leave today.

'I just have to get *them* settled somewhere before I go.' She nodded her head towards the dining room.

'You shouldn't have to think of all that at a time like this,' Ellie said. Her face was kind and soft.

What a pity she wasn't more reliable, Kate thought. 'I have to Ellie, these are the burdens of being a tycoon and running a goldmine like this.' Kate's voice was bitter. Everyone knew that it only broke even because she worked such long hours in the place.

'But couldn't somebody … ?'

'There *is* nobody. No money could pay anyone for looking after that lot.' Kate reached for the phone.

Ellie put out her hand to stop her.

'I'll do it,' she said.

'What?'

'It's only a week, Kate, you go to Mother.'

'You can't do it. They're a nightmare.'

'Don't I know it? But I'll do it for five times my normal wage.

Go on, Kate, you can't get a better deal than that.' Ellie was eager.

'What do you need all that money for?' Kate asked weakly.

'I thought I'd go to a spa for a makeover. Apparently Dan likes smaller, thinner, younger-looking girls, it turns out.'

'They *all* like smaller, thinner, younger girls, that's the system.' Kate's voice was clipped.

'Right, so it's all arranged, you go and see Mother, leave everything here to me.'

'I can't, Ellie.'

'Think of being on your knees to Rest Haven and Santa Rosa's and just *go!*' Ellie begged.

And Kate began to pack her case.

They were not at all pleased when they heard that Ellie was in charge.

'A *slattern* is what we would have called her in my time,' Donald sniffed.

'Not even a nurse, just a carer, a servant-class person,' said Georgia.

'I suppose she had a row with her boyfriend,' Heather said.

'At least she *had* a boyfriend, which is more than you ever had,' Hazel snorted.

Kate rang from the airport. 'I must have been mad,' she began. 'My mind is unhinged, otherwise I wouldn't have left them to you.'

'Thanks for the vote of confidence, Kate.'

'Don't alienate them. *Please*, Ellie. Woodlawns is all I've got. If they leave, we all go under ...'

'Safe journey.' Ellie hung up.

Ellie squared her shoulders and went in to face the inevitable grumblings. It was going to be hard enough to tolerate them over Christmas without the knowledge that the place was in worse financial condition than she had suspected.

'I suppose you think that you're going to skimp on the food and pocket the profit for yourself,' Donald said, his face purple already at the very thought of it.

'If she ate less, she wouldn't have lost her boyfriend,' Heather said.

'Tell us how *you* would know what a boyfriend might like,' Hazel snapped.

'This is the last Christmas I spend here,' said Georgia. 'Really, Kate Harris has gone too far, letting the staff go off and putting a carer in charge ...'

'At least they have a cook in Santa Rosa,' Heather said.

'And they have people of one's own kind in Rest Haven, they don't let dross in,' Donald said in a very definite allusion to the fact that Georgia was barred from there.

Ellie suggested that they might all like to eat at one table in the dining room, since there were only four of them. They looked at her glacially and said they were fine as they were. So she carried each individual dish to the different tables, thinking all the time about the wonderful, expensive spa treatment she would have.

She was only twenty-seven – not seriously old, but she would look twenty when all this seaweed and pummelling was over. Dan would wonder why he had ever been slow to commit to her.

Dan.

Would she and Dan ever grow old and difficult like these four sad, crabbed people here?

Of course not.

Once they had this early hiccup sorted out, they would grow old together, full of hope and adventure and satisfaction – wouldn't they? But maybe all these people sitting in the dining room of Woodlawns had thought that once. She watched them sniping at each other, sneering and criticising and laughing little hollow empty laughs of victory over nothing.

All around them the world was gearing up for Christmas. What a waste. What a despairing and pointless waste. She kept her views to herself every time Kate rang.

'They're all just fine,' she lied. 'How is Mother?'

'She's doing very well,' Kate would lie to her. 'No, not very much movement or speech yet, but she's coming along well …' And they would both end the conversations a little consoled.

At least Mother wasn't actually dying.

At least Woodlawns hadn't yet burned to the ground.

But it was getting increasingly hard for Ellie to keep her temper. She went in to the morning room late one evening because she heard someone playing the piano. There was Donald lost in a world of his own music, eyes closed. She watched him astounded, but he sensed her presence and threw a hard-edged book at her, shouting that she shouldn't creep up on people.

Georgia went out in the snow without a coat and fell on her face. Ellie had to get her back to her room, remove the turban she always wore and get her into a hot bath. Georgia ordered Bombay Sapphire Martinis all the time and complained at the lack of olives.

Heather told Ellie that no post or mail was to be delivered to Hazel, everything had to come to her.

'But if it's addressed to Hazel …?' Ellie began.

'You give it to *me!*' Heather had said, her eyes so narrow they were almost slits.

And then at dinner Donald started to flick the peas off his knife so that they landed on Georgia's table. And Georgia retaliated by throwing an entire plate of food back at Donald. Hazel and Heather gathered up their food and retreated to the corner of the dining room twittering in a panic.

Ellie's heart felt heavy. She had in her hands the future of four people, one eighth of Kate's clientele. They would all leave. Possibly during Christmas, with maximum publicity involving television coverage. Ellie could see Donald giving interviews and waving his stick as he crossed the road to Rest Haven. She could literally see the interview as if it had already happened, and she could see Kate's face, too, when she found out what had happened.

And at that moment, after several days of heroic self-restraint, Ellie lost it.

She put down the apple tart and ice cream on the sideboard and stood hands on hips looking at them all.

'I want you to know that I have had enough,' she began.

'*You* have had enough? What possible interest is that to us?' Donald asked.

'Excuse me, you are a paid person, paid to look after us,' Georgia explained.

'I wish the real Miss Harris was back,' Hazel began.

'Miss *Kate* Harris wouldn't make these entirely unsuitable scenes,' Heather nodded, agreeing with her sister for once.

'You call this a scene?' Ellie said, eyes blazing. 'Believe me, you haven't seen anything yet.'

They looked at her surprised. This wasn't her usual style.

'You are the most horrible people I have ever met in my whole life,' she said. 'There isn't an ounce of niceness in this room, but do I care? No I do *not* care. You could have fine lives, you could have friends, you could have family. You all have nice furniture in your rooms, you have people here to look after you all the time, you never say *please* or *thank you*. You are so horrible that people have left Woodlawns because of you. You come and sit in the hall complaining about the place whenever poor Kate is trying to show new arrivals around. You wake me at six in the morning asking for lightly boiled egg and toast soldiers, you disturb me when I am getting the dinner by asking for an extra-dry vodka Martini, you lay down the law about who is to get mail and who isn't.

'You have me dragging around from one table to another in a big dining room. You won't let me put up decorations for Christmas like half the world because it's vulgar or common or something. You have never once asked how our mother is. Not *once*.

'This place will close, you know, obviously it will have to. And you are the cause of it, yes, you four did it together. Well done.

'But it's a bit of an own goal, isn't it? It's *your* home that you are destroying. Where will *you* go when this place is sold? Half of you are barred from Rest Haven and Santa Rosa and when the word gets out – as it will – you'll *all* be barred.

'You will end up in some institution, some place smelling of piddle. And it's your own bloody fault.

'I'd love to know where you are going to go, yes, I really would. But in the end I suppose I'll forget you, all of you, and how you wrecked this Christmas for me and for Kate and for yourselves.

'Now I am going to take this apple tart out to the kitchen and eat it there and to hell with the lot of you.' And she banged the door with a mighty crash as she left the room.

They stared at each other, stunned.

For once none of them could think of anything to say.

In the kitchen Ellie had a large helping of apple tart and ice cream. The telephone rang: it was Kate. She sounded tired, but Mother was definitely recovering, all the feeling had returned to her right side.

'Dare I ask how they all are in Woodlawns?' Kate's voice was not strong. Ellie decided to let her have a night's sleep.

'Oh, you know, the usual,' she said.

'You are marvellous, Ellie, you are a saint. That's the only word for you.'

Ellie knew there would eventually be other words. But not tonight. She had a large brandy in her coffee. And then an even larger one without her coffee; and then, without going back into the dining room to clear up, she went upstairs to bed.

She woke when the light came in her window. God, what time was it? It was way after nine. Normally she served their breakfasts at 8 a.m.

Ellie brushed her teeth and rinsed with a mouthwash in case she still smelled of brandy, then she scrabbled into her clothes.

The door to the dining room was open. She saw that the dishes from last night had been removed. And they were all sitting at the same table. A plate of toast and a pot of tea had been prepared.

They were obviously coping.

She must now try to act normally. Maybe this thing could be saved.

'Eggs anyone?' she asked cheerfully.

They shook their heads. No, thank you, they were perfectly

fine. This was said in normal, civil tones. There were no nuances, no sneers.

Ellie felt the whole world tilt slightly. They couldn't possibly intend to ignore her outburst last night. That was too wildly unlikely to consider.

Heather cleared her throat. 'We were wondering if perhaps you would like to bring in *your* cup of tea and join us,' she said.

'Sure I will,' Ellie said. She felt a hollow in her stomach. This was it. They were going to deal with her all together. Well, she had to face it sometime. She sat with a bright smile on her face.

Georgia was now the spokesperson.

'We've been discussing things and we think we will all write to people we know to tell them how good this place is,' she said. 'And another thing, we realise that it's Christmas time,' she said firmly.

Ellie looked around her wildly. 'Yes, um … it is indeed Christmas time,' she said eventually.

'So perhaps we should all go shopping in town,' Georgia said. 'And buy a turkey, even?'

Ellie had already offered them a turkey for Christmas and they had all laughed in derision. Hazel and Heather wanted goose or nothing. Donald said he liked only guineafowl. And Georgia said she would prefer a couple of dozen oysters and otherwise couldn't summon up any interest.

So Ellie had planned a steak-and-kidney pie. But this looked like an olive branch and she must be seen to accept it.

'A turkey!' she exclaimed, as if she would never have thought of such a thing. 'Wouldn't that be lovely?'

Donald said that he thought a Christmas tree might be suitable and Heather and Hazel wondered could they go to a carol service when they went out. With her head still reeling, Ellie got Kate's old car out and they headed for the town.

Georgia immediately bought crackers and fairy lights, and negotiated with a young man to deliver a tree that afternoon. Heather and Hazel went round the turkey stalls prodding at the breasts of dead birds with all the expertise of farmers' wives. Donald went to an off-licence and explained to anyone who would listen that he had found drink a good servant but a poor master, so he did not imbibe now, but still he was buying for four ladies so he wanted to get something chateau-bottled and from a good year.

Ellie went around buying whatever else might be needed, keeping an eye on all of her very mad companions.

She lost Georgia first. Running up and down, revisiting the places she had been, she began to panic. She saw a pub door swing open and envied the lucky people who were not in charge of certifiable lunatics like she was, people who could go and have a wintry lunchtime drink.

From inside she heard a voice singing

'I like New York in June
How About You?'

There was something familiar about the voice, so she went back to look. There was Georgia sitting on the bar conducting the entire clientele in a sing-song. Then she actually *stood* on the bar for the crescendo. Her legs were still very good, Ellie noted. Legs and cheekbones did it all the time. Georgia had the place in the palm of her hand.

Amazingly, Georgia did not fall but was helped down to huge

applause. Ellie got her out as strangers patted her on the back and said she was wonderful.

'I wish the others could have heard you,' Ellie said. But Georgia was too busy smiling at her fans to reply.

They all had hot dogs and loaded the car and Ellie found them a carol service. Donald told the clergyman that they were from an old people's hotel and would love some of the young people in the parish to come and help them smarten the place up a bit and a date was fixed.

When they got back to Woodlawns, the Christmas tree was arriving and it had begun to snow again. They laughed like children and threw snowballs at each other. By now it seemed that they had never eaten at any other table than the one they all shared together.

When they had finished supper they decorated the tree. Donald told them that he had been without alcohol for nine years now. They murmured their admiration, but his eyes were sad.

'It wasn't soon enough,' he said. 'I was such a fool, didn't see how much I was losing.'

'What did you lose?' Ellie asked.

'My wife, my job, my self-respect.'

'Did your wife die?' Ellie hardly knew where she got the courage to ask him.

'Yes, yes, she died.'

Georgia put out her hand and laid it on his. 'Maybe she thought it was a good life, the life she had with you,' she said. *Georgia?* Saying something *nice?*

'And you must have been very interesting company,' said Heather.

'What with being a judge and everything,' agreed Hazel. The sisters *agreeing?*

These were strange times.

They talked on until late in the evening. Georgia said that her career had not been as successful as she might have liked. She often looked back and wondered had she sacrificed two perfectly good husbands for nothing.

'I wouldn't say it was for nothing – I bet they wouldn't say that!' Donald was gallant.

Heather and Hazel talked about Mummy and Daddy but not in the usual idolising way.

'They were a little old-fashioned,' Heather said.

'And thought they were right, no matter what,' Hazel agreed.

'And Hazel *did* have a boyfriend,' Heather said.

'But Daddy said he wasn't suitable,' Hazel said sadly.

'So that's why they made Hazel give the baby away, you see,' Heather explained.

Everyone saw and they were saddened by it.

'But he might still get in touch one day,' Hazel said hopefully and they all cheered up again.

They planned the next day. They would dress up for dinner. Ellie looked out the clothes she had been going to wear at Christmas with Dan. How extraordinary that she hadn't thought of him all day!

Later, when she was fixing Georgia's nightcap, which tonight was a Brandy Alexander, she told Georgia that she thought she might be getting over Dan.

'I do hope so, my dear, you are much too attractive for a man who goes *honk-honk* in his car,' Georgia said. 'Ellie, do you think I could let anyone see my hair tomorrow, instead of wearing the turban?'

'I'll cut and style it for you,' Ellie offered. She ironed Donald's dress shirt and she helped the sisters decide which stoles to wear. And there was a huge excitement when they all assembled.

Donald was resplendent in full evening wear, Heather and Hazel wearing the entire contents of their jewellery boxes; and eventually Georgia making her entrance down the stairs with her shining silver hair, and her classic black dress.

Kate rang during dinner. Georgia answered the phone.

'Ellie? Yes, I think she's sober enough to talk to you, she's been pouring brandy over the pudding. Will someone call Ellie? It's Kate on the phone. Oh, and Kate, how is your mother? She is? Good. Good. Well, we'll all see her when you bring her back here. You will be bringing her back with you, won't you?'

Ellie took the phone. They could only hear her side of it and had to guess what Kate was saying.

'No, of course not, perfectly sober, everyone, all of us. Yes, of course. And you'll be bringing Mother back, won't you? Oh, and Kate, everyone here has written letters to all their friends to encourage them to come and stay in Woodlawns. Oh, and another thing, a lot of boy scouts are coming on Friday to paint the fences and make window boxes. Will you be back while the tree is still up?

'The Christmas tree, Kate, it looks lovely. We are all perfectly all right, don't keep asking me how I feel. I feel just fine. No, he hasn't been in touch, but that isn't important. Love to Mother from me and from everyone here. Bye Kate ...'

Just then there was a honking sound in the avenue. Dan had come to see her on Christmas Day. Ellie went to the hall door. All the others went to the door of the dining room to listen.

He didn't even get out of the car. 'Come to take you for a drive honey,' he called. 'Can you get your coat and come with me now?'

'Happy Christmas, Dan,' Ellie said.

'Hey, honey, what kind of an answer is that? Is it a yes or a no?' He held his head on one side as he used to do, it used to drive her wild then.

'It's geriatric-speak for goodbye, Dan,' Ellie called and closed the door.

In the dining room they all hugged each other and scurried to sit down at the table again before she came back. Donald played the piano for them afterwards, just as he had that time when Ellie had found him. With his eyes closed, and his face very chiselled and handsome. And Georgia sang for them and told them tales of the music hall, mainly tales where everything had gone wrong. Heather said that she always asked for the mail in case Hazel's son might get in touch and she would go away, and Hazel said in amazement that she would *never* go away from Heather, never in a million years ...

Ellie knew that some day, quite soon, she would leave here and go and find a proper life. But in the meantime there was plenty to do to supervise the scouts and to get her mother and sister home. And very often the less explanation there was for anything the better ...

Christmas Timing

This would be their fifth Christmas together, or not together. But the principle was the same. Chris hated the smugness of married people who went on and on about anniversaries, as if a thing could only be celebrated when it was legit. She couldn't believe that her friends didn't know that she and Noel had got together in the winter five whole years ago. A magical winter when they kept finding out how much they had in common; they were both Christmas babies, one called Chris, one called Noel in deference to the season. They had both been bored rigid by the Olympic Games and never wanted to hear of a decathlon, a javelin, or a discus ever again. They had loved the same films and felt that at just touching thirty they were a little too old for nightclubbing.

On their first date they heard Stevie Wonder's 'I Just Called To Say I Love You'. Chris would never forget that as long as she lived. And the way Noel *did* call to say he loved her, from every phone box, hotel foyer, railway station. And from the family home whenever his wife was out of earshot.

The children had been so young then. Noel's children. And

of course, to be fair, his wife's children. They were very young, they were seven and eight. That was young. And oddly, as the years went by, they still seemed to be young. Chris couldn't understand it, everything else changed. But those children of Noel's were still clinging toddlers expecting him home, needing to be telephoned, wanting presents, demanding postcards daily on the few occasions when Noel and Chris *did* manage to get away together. They seemed to be getting younger in their photographs too. Or else dressing younger and assuming babyish positions. They were twelve and thirteen now. Why did they still get photographed cuddled up to Daddy, leaning on him, needing protection? Did a devilishly cunning wife always manage to snap them this way, knowing that these would be the pictures that got shown rather than complete family scenes?

They were very sensitive with each other, Chris and Noel. He never mentioned aspects of the family Christmas that might upset her, the parties for relatives and neighbours. She was the same with him, she never talked about how her parents always invited her father's junior partner, a man who had the huge advantage of being single. She never told him how her sisters talked to her darkly about the biological clock ticking away and how liberation was all very well but did one want to put off babies for ever?

In fact Chris thought that they were much more courteous to each other and anxious not to offend than were most married couples she knew. She often did those quiz-type articles in magazines. 'Are you compatible?' In all of them, answering honestly, she thought they came out with top marks. They always listened, fascinated, to stories of the working day. They never slouched around the house in slovenly and unattractive gear. Neither of them would dream of turning on a television

rather than having a conversation. They were tender and giving in their lovemaking rather than selfish. They didn't need to
cheat. They were compatible.

Sometimes she did an 'Are you romantic?' test. And they
were, they were!

He brought her a single flower, he remembered what she
wore and praised it. She always served dinner on a table, no
trays on the lap in Chris's flat.

And it was the same in the 'Is he a chauvinist pig?' tests. He
wasn't, he wasn't. With her hand on her heart she could say that
he admired her mind, thought her job was worthwhile, asked
her advice about his own, treated her equally in all things. There
was no way she could be considered his little bit of fluff.

There were no tests she shied away from. Not even the
'Will your love survive?' She went through it remorselessly and
decided that it would. Triumphantly, when all others had fallen
or cooled down. They had all the right ingredients for survival.
They were clear-sighted, they knew the limitations and yet could
travel to the furthermost boundaries. Even the regular Christmas
promise that next year they would be together. Properly. That
wasn't a weak link in their love. It was a necessary pronouncing
of commitment.

Noel loved doing these little psychological tests too.
Sometimes he found more that Chris hadn't seen in manage-
ment magazines. 'Is your love life suffering because of stress?'
They would laugh confidently and agree that Noel's love life
with Chris was doing nothing of the sort. He found a serious
one called 'Are you a cheat?' They went through it very carefully
and decided that he wasn't, because nobody was being let down.
And that when the time was right everything would be out in
the open.

So they had no fear of any Christmas Quiz dreamed up in a family newspaper to keep the readers happy and partially alert over Christmas. And though they were separated by many miles, they wouldn't be unhappy on Christmas Day. Noel had a picture of Chris sitting down in her family home surrounded by sisters and brothers-in-law, nephews and nieces, and good old family friends. He could imagine her sitting by the fire and picking up this marvellous questionnaire and filling it in quietly, smiling to herself in the knowledge that he, too, would be doing it by his fireside and that everything they answered to the questions would be almost word for word the same. Chris thought of Noel, after all the family fun with those two children who seemed to have reversed the ageing process, possibly getting rattles and soft toys in their stockings this year. He would ask for a little peace for Daddy to read the papers and it would be given to him. She could see him nodding and smiling over the kind of thing that might have other couples riddled with anxiety. Compatible, romantic, clear-sighted, non-chauvinist, non-cheating? They would win in every category. At around the same time on a crisp, cold afternoon on the day that was both Christmas and the day they had reached half of three score and ten, they sat down to do the Christmas Quiz.

This year it was in a different format. Not the usual boxes to tick for Yes and No and Possibly. Not the usual scoring scheme at the end: 'If you scored over 75 you are ridiculously happy,' or 'If you scored under 20, are you *sure* this relationship is for you?'

This year it was a completely new departure. You had to write in words, sentences, not ticks and crosses. There was no scoring at the end, only the suggestion that you leave the newspaper around the house so that the loved one could read it. That's if you wanted the loved one to change. Deep in their armchairs miles from each other, Chris and Noel, the thirty-five-year-old Christmas babies, nestled in to do the questionnaire. It was called 'Those little irritations', and under a whole lot of different headings you had to fill in the things about the loved one that caused you to wince. BE HONEST the headline screamed at you, and said there was no point in doing it unless you did it honestly.

In the house where Chris sat, children played with their new games by the tree, her sisters talked of new arrivals in the new year, her parents slept contentedly in their chairs. Her father's junior partner, who had the merit of being single, mended the Christmas lights and put batteries into all the gadgets that had been gift-wrapped without them. He saw Chris take up the questionnaire.

'Only a couple who were seriously mad would attempt that,' he said genially.

Chris looked at him pityingly. He must not know about her happy love life in case he ever let it slip to her parents.

'Oh that's right, only us singles would dare to do it. Fantasy life and all that.'

He smiled at her; he looked kind of different this year, perhaps he, too, had a secret life. She drew the paper up to her closer so that she could begin without his seeing the pure contentment on her face.

In Noel's house the children had gone out with their friends; they said there was nothing to do at home and now that they had opened their presents, couldn't they please go up the hill and fly kites like everyone else. Noel's wife talked excitedly with her father and mother about the business she was going to start. Yes, of course it would mean a bit of travel, but the children were well grown-up now and nothing made youngsters as independent as having to look after themselves a little in these formative years.

Noel opened the paper and smiled at 'Those little irritations'. He knew before he started that there would be no irritations, little or large, about his life with Chris.

Now, if it had been a questionnaire about him and his wife. Aha, *that* would be a different matter altogether! Look at the very first question.

'Does the loved one have any one phrase said over and over that drives you mad?' Chris hadn't. She was forever fresh and new in everything she said. But his wife, if she said 'Let's face it' once a day she must say it four hundred times. And her other phrase was 'To be strictly honest'. God, how he could scream when she said that. She always felt the need to say that she was being strictly honest when she told him the most trivial detail, like how long she had waited for a bus or what time somebody had telephoned. 'No, to be strictly honest it was at three o'clock she phoned, not half-past two, but let's face it, she does phone every day.' No, there was nothing at all in that category that he could hang on Chris. His wife, however, had another phrase that he hated. It was 'Right?' Said as a question after the most banal statement. 'I saw the new next-door neighbour today. Right?' Why did she say 'Right?' With an effort Noel dragged himself away from this bubbling rage. The quiz was meant to be about him and Chris, for heaven's sake, and so far she had passed with flying colours. Now on to question two. 'Is there any item of clothing that the loved one wears which you would like to consign to the dustbin?' Well, yes of course, that hideous mink cravat, and the line of chat that went with it. 'I don't approve of killing animals for their fur, but mink are different, they're vermin, *and* they've never known freedom.' But wait, that wasn't Chris, that was his wife. Chris wouldn't wear any kind of fur, nor would she have a list of excuses ready if she did. She wore lovely soft colours, grey-blue like her eyes and lilac sometimes, then when he would least expect it she might appear in a scarlet dress, or a yellow sweater. No, nothing for the dustbin there. He sighed with pleasure as he thought of his luck in love. A girl who never said a word astray or wore a garment that he didn't love.

In another house Chris was Being Honest, as the headline had urged her to be. Any phrase, over and over? Well, only the way he *always* said 'I must go to the little boys' room' when they went out to dinner, or even when they had dinner in her flat. But that wasn't something you hated. Just a bit predictable. Oh, and of course he always said 'Ice and slice?' when he got her a gin and tonic, as if it were mint new. But that was sort of a joke, he had imaginary quotation marks around it. No, she wouldn't write it down, that would be nit-picking. Across from the fire she saw her father's partner. She thought he had been looking at her, but she must have imagined it, he was very busy installing new batteries. He had brought a seemingly endless supply of them, which was good thinking on the part of someone who didn't have any children of his own. Chris read on. Was there an item of clothing belonging to Noel that she would throw out, apart from the underpants with the words 'Hot Stuff' on them? Well, there was the red-and-white-striped nightcap that had been funny once, and the fur hat after the Gorbachev cult, and the socks with sandals in the summer, and the driving gloves that were perfectly reasonable gloves in themselves but looked self-important on a steering wheel somehow. But these weren't real irritations. Not in the sense of being able to find a list of them.

There were twenty questions in the list. Twenty times Noel found at least five flaws in his wife and not one in his girlfriend. When Chris answered the twenty questions, however, she found twenty flaws in Noel. Twenty times, with tears beginning to start at the back of her eyes. Yes, she had found three unpleasant eating habits, and yes, she had observed two signs of corporate dishonesty, as well as an alarming six signs of petty personal meanness. She wrote none of them down. She didn't need to. It wasn't a paper to be left around to improve his habits. It was an eye-opener. As the scales fell from her eyes so did the glory seem to fall from Noel. She knew he would call soon and sing the Stevie Wonder lines down the phone. She knew she wouldn't tell him now that she knew he would never leave his home for her and furthermore she didn't want him to. It would be an ease to him too. He wasn't a basically bad man, just a basically irritating one.

In another house, Noel had counted seven unpleasant eating habits in his wife, and such high levels of corporate dishonesty that he feared she would be in a major criminal league when she got her business going. Noel knew that this was the time he would tell his wife that he wanted to leave. He would tell her today, this very day. It would be fairer and she could go ahead with her plans without taking him into consideration. He hadn't realised just how far they had grown apart. Just how little his children needed him. What a revelation it had been.

He would tell her straight out and then phone Chris. And this time, no need to go up to the bedroom saying he needed to go to the little boys' room to make the call. No need to go down the road to the phone box on the corner. He would be honest.

Noel could hardly wait to know what Chris would say. Perhaps she would leave home immediately and drive back to her flat in the city. What would there be for her to stay at home for? He would drive around to see her, take a bottle of tonic, possibly, and a lemon, she'd have gin, it would be silly to duplicate but he did know how she loved a gin and tonic with its ice and slice.

He wished he could see her now. But later, afterwards, he would ask her what it had been like in the hours before he had rung to tell her that he was free.

Chris sat and played a game of electronic ice hockey with the friend of the family, her father's partner, who happened to be single and who also happened to be very nice.

They were the only ones who heard the telephone ring, and he agreed with her that there was no point in answering it. Only very irritating people rang on Christmas Day.

Christmas Present

Christmas was coming: the lights had gone up everywhere. Santas appeared in the shops, and the threatening notices about Ordering Turkeys In Advance had appeared in every butcher's window. Mam had ordered theirs. Joe checked several times.

'Oh, Joe, if you ask me again, I'll get into the oven and baste myself on Christmas Day. Of course I've ordered one. And whatever it is, it'll be wrong.'

She was right, Joe agreed resignedly. On Christmas Eve his granny and his grandfather came, and somehow the day went downhill the moment they arrived. They weren't married to each other, these grandparents – they didn't even like each other. Granny was Mam's mother and seemed to think Mam would have lived in a smarter house in a classier way if she hadn't married Dad. And Grandfather was Dad's father, and he was bad-tempered about everything and said that people's values had changed and the world wasn't what it used to be.

Joe's mam and dad even started to fight with each other, which they didn't do for the rest of the year. Each year they thought it was going to be fine, but then, a couple of days before, the rot would set in. Joe was only ten and he could see it coming. His parents were very old, why couldn't they spot it like a black cloud on the horizon?

'It's getting grand and Christmassy, Mam,' he'd said, about three days before.

'You'd know it was, your father's started singing that song again.' Her mouth was in a grim line. It was a song his dad had heard on the radio:

> *I'll scream if I hear White Christmas*
> *Just once more on the radio,*
> *And since I've been grown up*
> *Each time it's shown up*
> *I've gone and thrown up in the snow ...*

Joe thought it was great too. Mam didn't. She loved Bing Crosby and what's more her *parents* loved Bing Crosby and this was making a mock and a jeer of everything that was important.

Dad bought paper napkins with jokes on them.

'They might liven up the Night of the Living Dead around our table,' he had said.

Mam said that her mother thought that a Christmas meal without linen napkins was more or less like sitting down and eating chips out of a newspaper.

'Something that you and I did a lot when we were courting and you loved me,' Dad said.

'I still love you, you big fool,' Mam said, but her heart wasn't in it. It was like being on automatic pilot.

Joe asked his friend Thomas if it was the same in his house. It wasn't: there were so many of them in Thomas's house, dozens of them. There were never enough presents, and people were always giving things for the wrong ages. Even the wrong sexes. Thomas got a night-dress case shaped like a crinoline lady once. They had put it in the kennel and the dog had eaten the head off it and got sick.

'But do they fight, your Ma and Da?'

Thomas thought about it. 'They roar,' he said, 'but not more than usual.' That wasn't much help.

Joe wished that Grandfather and Granny wouldn't come, they were the cause of the whole thing. If it were just themselves they'd have a great time. If his grandparents weren't there they could watch what they liked on television and maybe he could go round to Thomas's house or Thomas could come to his. And Mam and Dad would sit and laugh and say, 'Do you remember this?' and 'Do you remember that?' and they always seemed to remember good things.

Grandfather remembered times when people had heart. And Granny remembered the style and the quality that used to come to their house years ago when things were different. And both memories seemed to cast everyone into gloom.

'What would you like best for Christmas ... not a present, not a million pounds, but just for something to happen?' Joe asked his mam.

'I'd like your father to quit singing that send-up of "White Christmas",' she said.

'What would you like best, Dad?'

'I'd like your mother to stop play-acting with decanters and putting name places on the table for five people and calling a jug a sauceboat,' he said. Joe's fears were confirmed. The Christmas hostility had settled.

What was the very worst thing about their coming? The complaints. The snide remarks. The things they saw and heard that displeased them. He couldn't put sticky paper over their mouths. What a pity they had to see and hear so much. Granny did most of the seeing.

'I see you have plastic flower tubs,' she would say, 'what a pity, what a great pity,' and she would sigh a sigh that went to the very fibre of her being. And everyone would get downcast over the huge descent in standards that had come over the family since Mam had married Dad and gone down to the level of plastic flower pots.

Grandfather said that the music nowadays was intolerable. That there was never a tune in anything like there was in the old days, just fellows shouting and straining and no talent at all. If he had a voice he would sing the songs of the old days. But he hadn't. The company felt somehow to blame because Grandfather didn't have a voice to sing with. And as for that mad dog of theirs, barking and yelping, or the studio audiences in any funny show cackling inanely ...

It was a wonder Grandfather wore a hearing aid if he didn't like what he heard. And Granny wore those pebbly glasses to see things she didn't like.

An idea came to Joe.

They arrived on Christmas Eve.

Everything was wrong, of course, as it always was. Granny talked about the journey to this part of the world as if where they lived was some kind of penal settlement far from civilisation as she knew it.

Grandfather said he had come in a train full of alcoholic louts with cans of lager shouting and singing and playing their music at a high volume.

Joe couldn't put his plan into practice yet. So he endured Christmas Eve night as he always had. The settling in – Grandfather finding the fact that there was traffic on the road a grave setback. Granny saying that the house was so small it was amazing that they didn't all fall over each other.

Christmas morning they all went to church – and, oh dear, that had all changed like so many things, for the worse.

Then they came home and had breakfast. Joe's Mam and Dad were beginning to get edgy with each other as they did every year. Dad was humming 'White Christmas' under his breath.

'If you sing, I'll use the carving knife for a purpose which its makers didn't intend,' Mam said through gritted teeth. She was looking at the linen napkins.

'If you fold them and put them in glasses so that we have to take them out again before we can have a drink, I'll insert one of those things down somebody's throat,' Dad said in an undertone.

Joe watched his grandparents like a hawk. He had to be ready to make his move when an opportunity presented itself.

It happened when they were opening presents.

Granny got some awful handkerchief sachet sent to her by a friend who was called the Honourable Something. Granny was overcome by the generosity of this ridiculous present. She stroked it and eventually took off her glasses to wipe her eyes at the emotion of such a tasteful and aristocratic gift.

Joe plunged quickly.

He knocked her glasses from the table where she had placed them, so they fell behind her. Then he engineered that she lean forward for a moment to look at some antic of the dog. She looked without much interest or pleasure or indeed vision, and then she sat back heavily and crunched her glasses to little pieces.

There was an enormous fuss, dustpans and brushes were got. Granny was consoled. New glasses could be got, but not, of course, until after the holidays. Not until opticians went back to work. There was much sympathy and huge confusion. How had this happened?

'I'm normally so careful,' Granny said.

Joe was sympathetic. Polite.

Out in the kitchen he heard father say, 'Well, she won't be able to turn the plates upside down and see if they're bone china this year.'

Joe's mother said, 'She's still got her hearing, she'll hear if you sing that song about White Christmas.'

But there wasn't the same bad temper as usual.

Joe watched his grandfather. Sometimes he took his hearing aid out, often to look at it to turn it up or down. Why wasn't he doing it now?

Switch, the big, lovable, near-Labrador usually lay stretched happily in front of the fire, but at Christmas he always absented himself, so Joe had to keep dragging him back into the sitting room. Switch had been born on some day years and years ago, when Ipswich were playing Arsenal, and his dad always said wasn't it great that Ipswich won ...

Grandfather got an alarm clock for a Christmas present. He listened for the tick and couldn't hear it properly so, as he often did, he removed his hearing aid to test it.

'Get it, boy,' Joe said, and the dog snapped at the small bit of plastic. He chewed it happily, delighted with the new toy and mangled it out of any recognisable shape.

In an attempt to retrieve it, Joe made sure that all the wires were wrenched from it. Grandfather was astounded. He hadn't heard his grandson's cry of encouragement. Neither had anyone else. Or if they had, it wasn't mentioned.

The Christmas lunch appeared on the table. As always, it seemed great to Joe – dish after dish appeared. His grandmother didn't pick them up to read what was written underneath.

'That smells very nice,' she said instead. Joe's mam nearly dropped the turkey. Every other year there had been sorrowful reminiscences of the times when Christmas was Christmas and the bird had been brought in on a silver salver. Now, since she couldn't see the plate it was resting on, there was nothing to trigger off a trip down Memory Lane.

Dad was carving. 'And a leg for you, Father?' Dad came over and placed it in front of him and looked at him as if waiting for approval.

'That looks very good, son,' Grandfather said.

From the other room the sounds of the Chieftains belting out their numbers. Everyone's foot was tapping including Granny's; it had been a good choice, it sort of spanned the generations. Grandfather didn't hear it at all. Nor did he hear Switch yowling in time to the music.

There was a marvellous film on television on Christmas Night. Dad had said they wouldn't be able to have it, because his father would say that the values were all wrong … fellows not fighting for their country like fellows should, and language that would make a soldier blush.

Granny would say that that sort of thing was fine in its place but not on Christmas Day when everyone had eaten a good dinner.

But this year? Maybe … ? Joe looked at his parents hopefully.

'Give it a lash,' said his father with good-humoured enthusiasm.

'The skies can't fall on us,' said Joe's mam.

As they watched the film, Grandfather looked for a while, pleased at the images and understanding nothing at all. Then he dropped off to sleep peacefully.

Granny sat in her chair seeing only a blur. But she liked the music and thought she followed the plot. Then she too went to sleep.

On the day after Christmas, Mam and Dad used always to have people in for a drink. The neighbours would come and say their heads were splitting and it had been the final blight on the festive season. Granny used to sniff and say that people of this sort had been the salt of the earth in their own place, but of course their own place had been at the back door.

Grandfather used to say that these people talked about money and drink and horses and football and had no values like people of old who talked of nationhood and identity.

This year his grandfather and grandmother sat benignly when the guests arrived. Drinks were handed to them. Clasps of goodwill were exchanged.

Joe saw his dad giving his mother a bit of a squeeze in the kitchen, as they went in to take more mince pies out of the oven. Granny couldn't see the paper plates and plain paper napkins. Grandfather couldn't hear the assembled company singing 'I'll scream if I hear White Christmas' as his dad conducted them.

'It might not be like this every Christmas,' his father said as the departure came the next day.

'No, indeed,' said Joe. He was sure he couldn't get away with it again.

'Not both of them anyway,' his mam said. She never knew, did she? Her eyes were bright.

Of course he couldn't immobilise both of them again. But

somehow the memory of them seeing nothing and hearing nothing had been a touching one. It made them less of the ogres they had been.

They would never be able to threaten his Christmas again.

The White Trolley

It had been a long hard year running the shop. Too many very early mornings, too many late nights. A lot of anxiety about introducing new lines. But the Patels had got it right. It was Christmas Eve and they knew that they had more than justified Uncle Javed's hopes for them. It was up and running now, their own place, in the middle of city offices. A place where they had the courage to stock much more than the usual sandwiches and fast food for office lunchers. They had even opened a gift section with small electronics, unusual stationery, little leather goods and gadgets of every kind.

The other shopkeepers had shaken their heads and said they were mad. But the Patels were newly married and fired with ideas, gently encouraged by the watchful Uncle Javed. The young couple had a gut feeling about the kind of service city workers needed and now, as they finally prepared to close for the Christmas holidays, the Patels stood and watched proudly as their most successful venture, white trolleys overflowing with carefully packed goods, waited in line to be collected.

These were goods that had been bought in the lunch hour

or during the day, when customers had been able to slip away from their offices. Each trolley had a name written on it with a big felt pen on cardboard. The customer showed the receipt and then pushed the trolley out the door. There was a chorus of greetings and good wishes and the Patels watched as a hundred different Christmases left their shop in trolleys. Uncle Javed congratulated them, remarking that there were many new faces among the regular customers.

Mr Patel was talking to one of the regulars when Uncle Javed gave the trolley marked S. White to a young, anxious looking woman with long hair falling into her eyes. Mrs Patel was outside in the cold, pointing towards a bus stop and giving directions, when Uncle Javed gave another trolley marked S. White to a stooped man with sad eyes. Then, under his mischievous gaze, the young couple closed their store and took the first proper rest they had known for over a year.

Sara White pushed the trolley to the van where Ken waited patiently. There was someone like Ken in every office, a man who didn't drink, who didn't seem to have any real life of his own, not one that he talked about, anyway. But who was always there, ready to help. It had become a tradition that Ken drove people home after the Christmas Eve office party. He piled all the carrier bags into the back of the van and returned the trolley to the little line. His three other passengers were still singing cheerfully as he dropped each of them to their homes and they seemed reluctant to leave.

Only Sara was sober and silent as she sat beside him in the front seat.

'You must have bought up the whole shop,' Ken said to her.

'Well, it's going to be a difficult Christmas this year, I want to make it different for them, not too traditional and all that,'

Sara said and looked out of the window at the crowds making their way home in the rain.

Sara's husband had left home in the springtime. Quite unexpectedly, apparently. She had spoken little of it in the office but some of the girls had told Ken that she cried a lot and always expected that he would phone and say he was coming back.

'I'm going to make them Thai Curry tomorrow. They'll like that and it won't be sort of reminding them, you know.'

'I know,' Ken said, even though he didn't.

He helped her into the house with the carrier bags. Last year there had been a tall thin man in a red sweater called David opening the door and, taking the bags for her, he had invited Ken in to have a drink. This time two children opened the door.

'You're very late,' the girl said disapprovingly.

'I suppose it was all stupid games and things at the party,' the boy said.

'You remember Ken.' Her voice was bright. Too bright.

'Yeah,' said the girl.

'Hi,' said the boy.

Ken said 'good night' sharpish. No thanks, he didn't want to come in. He wished everyone a very Happy Christmas.

'Well now,' Sara said.

'Well?' said Adam, who was thirteen and had come to the end of a bad day. All his friends seemed to be having proper Christmases, with presents and relations and trees and parties. Adam didn't know what he would do if his mother said once more in that false sort of accent she spoke with sometimes, that it was just a day … 'that's all Christmas was when you came to think of it, just a day'.

'Well?' said Katie who was twelve and missed her father with a dull sort of ache that never went away. Things would never be all right again. When they saw their dad he just sighed and groaned and cast his eyes up to heaven about their mother. Her mother couldn't speak of Dad without shaking and trembling and talking about that woman and all the trouble she had caused. Adam and Katie didn't talk about Dad at all. It was easier.

But nothing is easy at Christmas time. They watched as their mother's false smile tried to reach her eyes and didn't succeed.

'Well,' she said again. 'Let's see what we've got here.' And very slowly she began to unpack on to her kitchen table the entire Christmas shopping list of a Mr Stephen White. His credit card receipt was in one of the bags. A man who liked wrapped white sliced bread, and tins of peas and two portions of frozen turkey breast. A man who had bought ten tins of cat food, and four horrible, horrible little packages of talcum powder and soap with Merry Yuletide written on them. Unbelieving still, Sara opened bag after bag. Everything she hated most in the world was unfolding before her. Packet stuffing for a turkey! Could this man have intended to put some dry packet stuffing in a frozen breast of turkey? There were tins of made-up custard, there were convenience foods like she had never known. Things you boiled in a bag, things you stewed in a packet of sauce. Sara's eyes were round in horror.

Her face began to crumple, and for the first time since their father had left, the children saw that their mother was about to cry. Adam and Katie looked at each other in amazement.

She had never cried when Dad had walked away and gone off to live with that strange Mrs Hunter, the woman with the greasy hair and the long droopy cardigan. And here she was now about to collapse because of something to do with the shopping. Sara fought back the tears. She could not let herself go now, now of all nights. But it was eight o'clock on Christmas Eve. Some half-witted man called Stephen White in some other part of the city had the beautiful soft leather handbag she had bought for Katie, the tiny CD player with the ten carefully chosen discs that she had found for Adam. The pure silk scarf that would go with Katie's green eyes, the camera that Adam had always wanted.

This man, who ate white bread and frozen turkey breasts would have all the lemon grass, and black olives, fresh limes and coriander. He would have the fresh prawns, the designer salad ingredients, the superb cheese. Even if there *were* any other stores open now, which she doubted, Sara couldn't afford to buy anything else. She had spent half a month's salary in Patel's and they with their happy marriage and successful business had managed to ruin everything for her. Because of their incompetence she was going to have to serve this man's revolting food for Christmas. Or they would eat nothing at all.

She didn't deserve to be let down like this, she had worked so very hard and fought so very bitterly to have the children to herself this Christmas. She didn't want them going anywhere near David and that appalling Marjorie Hunter who looked as if she never washed her face or combed her hair.

David said it wouldn't be Christmas for him if he couldn't see the children at least for a little bit of the day. He had offered all kinds of things, he could collect them, he could visit them for an hour, he could send a taxi for them. He would be lonely, he said.

'You should have thought about that when you left them,' Sara had said crisply.

'Please Sara,' he had actually begged her.

'How could you possibly be lonely, David?' Sara had said. 'You have the lovely Marjorie Hunter to entertain you.' And he had hung up then. Defeated.

She saw both the children staring at her. Worried.

'Do you want us to put the shopping away?' Katie asked.

'I'll open the freezer,' Adam offered.

'This isn't the shopping,' Sara sobbed, her shoulders heaving. 'This isn't anyone's normal shopping, it's the shopping of a madman.' And with her head between the tins of cat food and the packets of instant whipped mousse, Sara White wept all the tears that the children had never seen her shed in this, the worst year of their lives.

They were entirely at a loss. For month after long month it had been a brittle, tense way of coping with Dad leaving. Katie had tried to talk, she had sat on her mother's bed and begged her to tell her what had happened. But she got no answer. Only that strange, unnatural laugh that didn't sound at all like her mother. Adam had wondered was it because he had got a bad school report? Could that have had anything to do with it? But again that laugh, he wasn't to be so silly to think that a bad report could make a father leave home.

They couldn't understand why she had never cried. The children could not understand that their mother was tormented with her own desperate questions and the person with the answers had simply walked away.

Katie and Adam hardly dared to touch the weeping woman with her head down on the table in the middle of this perfectly ordinary looking shopping. But, tentatively, Katie touched her mother's shoulder. Adam went and got a great lump of kitchen paper for her to dry her eyes. Gradually Sara sat up and looked at them. She blew her nose loudly and gave each of her children a squeeze.

'It's just the last straw, you see,' she explained.

They didn't see.

'I wanted it to be special for you,' she said humbly.

They huddled together and talked. She told them how much she loved them and how hard she had fought for them this Christmas. And now there were only terrible, terrible things to cook, and all their lovely presents gone for ever to this madman.

'I don't mind these things,' said Katie. 'You don't have to cook with them, we'll do it.' Katie waited for her mother to protest. But Sara took one glance at the alien food on her table and sighed heavily. Adam held his breath and followed his mother's gaze. At least she had stopped crying.

'This stuff's easy to cook,' he boasted. 'And we'll find the madman after Christmas and get our presents back.'

His mother touched his cheek. The small gesture surprised Adam and he felt happy. For the first time in months he and his sister did not seem like some impossible burden their mother had to suffer alone.

Warily, Sara watched her son and daughter play with the garish items that had been bought by Mr S. White. The tins and packets were being tossed carelessly between Adam and Katie; their faces getting increasingly excited as they invented elaborate names for the dishes on their Christmas Day menu; a meal of sorts seemed possible, Sara conceded. She looked at her children, both ridiculously pleased with themselves, and she felt blessed. They deserved their presents and she knew, she had always known, what they really wanted for Christmas.

'Would you like to call your dad?' she asked gently. The

children looked at her, their shoulders sagged slightly and they avoided her eyes. 'You can invite him to your lunch,' she added softly.

'Only if he brings some food and our presents,' said Katie too brightly.

'Don't be silly! He wouldn't come without Her!' Adam tried to hide his frustration but recently their lives had become so complicated.

'Daddy *could* bring her,' said Katie, hesitantly.

A furtive look passed between Katie and Adam; they hardly dared to hope.

Sara studied the shopping of Mr S. White with open suspicion. 'Do you really think you can manage this lot?'

Two eager faces beamed back at her.

'Easy,' said Adam confidently. Katie nodded her agreement.

Sara sighed. Her children were right, she thought, it was 'easy' and she went to the telephone. 'I will have to warn Daddy … and … Marjorie,' she said and smiled at the two impish faces, 'that it will be a light and very uncomplicated lunch.'

The Feast of Stephen

Stephen White had always liked the Patels who ran the great shop near his office. They were such a hard-working couple and yet they always had time to have a few words.

Mrs Patel had once advised him what to take to a colleague who was in hospital. Stephen White had been going to buy her chocolates, but the busy little woman in her sari said that she thought a packet of cards with envelopes would be better and then if he were to get her a book of stamps as well that would be perfection.

It had indeed been a highly acceptable gift. The woman in the hospital bed had been surprised at receiving something so thoughtful.

Foolishly Stephen told her it was the suggestion of the woman in the mini market. It seemed to diminish the gift but Stephen was such a fair-minded person he didn't want to take credit for an idea which was not his own. He had always been that way. Not pushy enough his father had said, but then nobody was pushy enough for Stephen's father who had eventually pushed himself into a situation where he was prosecuted for fraud.

Never stood up for himself his sisters had said, and Wendy the wife that he thought had loved him had left him because she said he would never light a fire under anyone, himself included.

Stephen hadn't known that he was meant to light fires under anyone. It hadn't been part of any original deal. He thought you went out and worked hard and earned money and stood behind other people in queues and waited your turn. He didn't know a new system had come in where you were meant to have a confrontation about everything, and not to back down and not to lose face.

And this, of course, was why he was in this situation just before Christmas time.

Redundant.

His boss had been embarrassed.

'There's no easy way to say this, Stephen, and no good time of year to say it either,' she had begun.

He had looked at her blankly.

'But of course you must have seen it coming,' she went on.

Stephen hadn't seen it coming. And not on Christmas Eve.

As they gave him his receipt they put his trolley away, having written S. White in large letters on cardboard for when he would collect it later.

They were really a highly efficient pair, they deserved their success. At that time, of course, Stephen thought he was a man with a job and a future.

Not so when he came back after the news of the afternoon. This time he was like someone on autopilot. It was his first Christmas alone, he just had to pick up his shopping and face it. For the last two years since Wendy had left him he had gone to his brother's house.

But they played a lot of games there, things you had to be quick-witted about. It wasn't easy or relaxed.

This year Stephen had thought he would make his own Christmas dinner, get two frozen turkey breasts, one looked so sad. And you never knew who might join you.

George in the office had said he might stroll by. Not a definite arrangement or anything but just a possibility. Stephen had wanted to be prepared. He would get nice easy foods like tins of custard and packets of mince pies. And some packet soups and stuffings, things you just had to add a little water to.

Small gifts for the ladies in the flats near him, they would like talcum powder and matching soap, he thought.

He bent sadly over the trolley and brought it out to his car.

He unpacked bag after bag, all of them with 'season's greetings' written on them. He stacked them neatly in the boot. He knew that he had bought far too much. George wouldn't stroll by, not tonight or tomorrow. You didn't stroll to the house of a man who had just been sacked. There would be nothing to say.

Grimly Stephen continued unloading his supplies. But he didn't really look at them. Otherwise he would have realised he had the wrong trolley. He was a person of regular habits, and permanent rituals.

Normally he would have stored anything for the freezer on one side and covered it with a rug for greater insulation.

But tonight he didn't make any distinction. And he headed out into the rainy night with tears on his face. Tears of failure as he drove the contents of Sara White's trolley to the small flat where he had lived since he and Wendy had sold what was always called the marital home.

Back at the office the party would be in full swing. He had always, in his quiet way, enjoyed it on other Christmas Eves. He found a background from which to observe it all, it had been good-natured if a little silly.

But this year they would all have been sympathising with him, assuring him he would get another job in no time. Better let them speculate about him behind his back, wonder how poor Stephen was taking it all.

He would come back after Christmas and tidy things up. He had been told that he need not leave until some time that suited him early in the New Year.

Stephen opened the first package and discovered prawns in their shells. Well now, he thought, the Patels were not as efficient as he had thought, they must have included a bag from someone else's trolley. Still, it was easy to do. He looked at the prawns, interested; they were so prehistoric . . . almost like dinosaurs really. He wondered who could possibly cook and eat such things. Then the next bag had a leather handbag and a green scarf. There were jars of olives, strange crusty bread with a herby smell. It took Stephen White five whole minutes to realise that he had none of his careful shopping, that in fact he had been given totally the wrong trolley.

But it had his name on it back in the store which was long closed now. And surely his credit card receipt must be in one of the bags. He rooted around to find it and there it was behind a miniature CD player that must have cost a fortune. But it was for Sara White, that's what she had signed.

Some crazed woman who must, by the amount of her bill and the look of her trolley, run an exotic restaurant and quite possibly a gift shop. What must she be thinking in some other part of the city as she looked for all these entirely inappropriate things that she had presumably assembled for herself and her family.

And how was he going to find her? The credit card people

wouldn't reveal her address. The Patels would be locked up and gone away.

Suddenly Stephen felt very tired and sad. He sat at the kitchen table loaded with such unexpected things; a big tear splashed down on the coconut milk. He would never find this Sara White in the phone book, there was no point even in looking, she might be there under her husband's name.

His Christmas was ruined because this *stupid stupid* woman couldn't take the right trolley. But that wasn't really why the tear had fallen, the food didn't matter. Stephen White sat weeping in the kitchen on Christmas Eve because at the age of 48 he was unemployed and his wife had been gone for three years and he had nobody and nothing to live for.

There was a loud banging on the door.

Stephen brushed his face and went to answer it. It was George from the office, with a bottle of wine and possibly quite drunk already.

'I was strolling by,' said George who lived in another part of the city entirely and had made the detour out of solidarity with the man who had just been sacked.

George was amazed at all the food. He examined all the ingredients.

'Imagine that. Well I don't believe it! You were going to make a Thai curry,' he said, full of admiration.

'Was I?' Stephen was bewildered.

'I must say I do admire you, Stephen, a few of us wondered would you be all right, you looked a bit grey this afternoon … wait until I tell them you were having a party.'

'A party?'

George laughed easily as he drew the cork from the bottle of wine he had brought with him.

'Well, don't tell me you were going to eat all this yourself! When's it going to start?'

'I don't know,' Stephen said.

It was all becoming increasingly unreal sitting here with George from the office drinking a full-bodied red wine at a table covered with some woman's fancy shopping, having been sacked from his job.

'What time did you tell them?' George wanted to know.

'I didn't tell them,' Stephen said.

George wasn't bothered by that. He refilled his glass.

'Well, they could come any time then,' he said in a brisk and businesslike way. 'Come on Stephen, we'd better get our skates on, start frying the mushrooms and onions.'

'But what for?' Stephen begged.

'Well as a base, then we fry the chicken, stir in the green paste and the coconut milk ...'

'We can't do this ...' Stephen was hoarse with fear.

'Well, of course, if you want to make the green curry for the prawns, well that's fine, we'll do a red one for the chicken.'

'But the people! I haven't asked anyone!' Stephen cried.

'Well definitely skates on then Stephen, we'd better go round asking them.'

And in front of Stephen's horrified eyes, George from the office, carrying a glass of red wine and most certainly under the weather from the office party, went across the corridor and banged loudly on the door of Mrs Johnson, pillar of the Residents' Association, undoubtedly the most difficult woman in the entire block of flats.

Stephen had bought her some talcum powder and a matching soap, hoping to get into her good books and that she wouldn't glare at him quite so much.

But, because of that appalling Sara White, whoever she was, he had *no* talcum powder for Mrs Johnson, he only had an inebriated colleague, well ex-colleague, hammering on the woman's door. Stephen felt slightly faint. And closed his eyes. When he opened them he saw to his amazement that Mrs Johnson seemed to be having a perfectly normal conversation with George. She was even asking him what kind of bottle she should bring.

'Anything at all really,' George was saying. 'Adds to the excitement.'

George said he would be back shortly, he had now got the names of other residents from Mrs Johnson and everyone would assemble in about an hour. They should have everything ready by then.

Stephen sat down beside the wreckage of the table and the greatly reduced wine bottle. This just couldn't be happening. It was all a dream, he had fallen asleep and just dreamed it all. That was it. Then he heard George's voice booming downstairs and excited cries coming from that quiet couple in Number Sixteen who hardly ever looked up from the pavement to talk to you. George had asked these people to Stephen's house and was planning to cook all Sara White's insane shopping list for them.

The phone rang.

He hardly felt strong enough to answer it but he picked it up. It was a woman's voice.

'Stephen?' she said.

'Yes,' he said bleakly.

'Stephen White?' she sounded doubtful.

'Oh, is that Sara?' he asked with real warmth in his voice. 'I'm so glad you rang.'

Now this terrible woman could come and take all her stuff and give him back what he wanted, what he had bought in fact.

'No.' The voice sounded disappointed. 'No, it's Wendy, actually, who's Sara?'

'Wendy!' He couldn't have been more surprised.

'Yes, well, season of goodwill and all that, I just thought I'd ring to see how you are.'

'I was sacked today as it happens.'

'Best thing that could have happened to you,' Wendy said. 'You were always too good for them, but you'd never leave. Now you can do something you'll enjoy.'

'Yes, well ...' Wendy was always very positive, no challenge too difficult for her.

'Are you depressed and moping about it alone at home?' she asked.

He thought for a moment. Wendy couldn't be doing all that much herself if she had called him.

'No, actually I'm having a party shortly,' he said.

'A *party*!' Wendy couldn't believe her ears.

'Yes, Thai curry, chicken and prawns,' he said proudly.

'Well, good for you.' She sounded grudging and astonished, and a little lonely.

'You're very welcome, I'd love to see you again, Wendy,' said Stephen White to his ex-wife.

'In about an hour's time, then, that would be great,' she said.

And George came back to say that it was shaping up as a fine party list, but they should really think of getting their skates on and as he had collected five different bottles already, perhaps they should open one for the sheer conviviality of it all.

The Civilised Christmas

It had been a civilised divorce, people said. What did that mean? It meant that Jen never said a word against Tina, the first wife, the beautiful wife who had run away and run back half a dozen times. It was civilised because Jen wrapped Stevie up in his scarf every Saturday and took him by two buses to Tina's house without complaining. She smiled an insincere smile as Tina, often in housecoat, always lovely, came to the door. Tina used to ask her in at one time, but Jen had always said no, thank you, she had some shopping to do. Tina would repeat the word 'shopping' in wonder, as if it were a very unfamiliar and outlandish thing for someone to do on a Saturday. When Stevie's visit was over, Tina put him in a taxi and Jen took him out of it and paid the taximan. Tina had a house, a terraced house, she had a three-piece suite with beautiful flowers on it, she had a mirror with a big gilt frame in her hall, but she never had the taxi fare home for her son.

They said it was civilised because Tina hadn't contested the custody. Her job took her away from time to time – she was a casino croupier and was often called on to go to big functions in the country. Her hours were unsuitable, much better not to try and rear an eight-year-old boy, better for the child. And anyway, the boy's father wanted the child so much, let's be civilised about it, Tina had said. Martin was so delighted that there was no battle, he had started to think almost warmly about Tina. Stevie loved going to see his beautiful mother and her bright chatty friends. It was all much better than the days when Mum and Dad had been fighting and crying. They had told him it would be better this way and they were right. Mum had bought him a computer, so usually he spent the time at that when he went to Mum's house. All the people had wine and sandwiches and they would come in and watch him and say wasn't he marvellous. Mum had a big bottle of apple juice all for him, as well as the sandwiches, and she used to ruffle his hair and say he was very brilliant as well as handsome, and that he would look after her in her old age when all her looks and her friends had gone.

Mum's friends would pat him on the back approvingly and it was all very grown-up and exciting. Mum even realised that he was old enough to take a taxi on his own. She would run lightly down the steps and whistle, a real ear-splitting whistle, and passers-by would smile as they always did at Mum.

At school people asked Stevie was it awful, his parents being divorced, and he said no, honestly, it was fine. He saw them both, you see, and they didn't fight, he was welcome in two places. And in the pub where Martin had his half-pint on the way home from work, the kind motherly woman who polished glasses and listened to life stories asked him if it was all working out and if the boy was settling down with his new mother. 'Uh, Jen isn't his mother,' Martin would say happily. 'Nothing is ever going to replace his real mother, he knows that, we all know that.' The woman smiled as she shone up the gleaming brass on the pumps and said it would be a happy world if everyone was as civilised as Martin and his wife.

This would be their first Christmas together. Jen, Martin and Stevie. Jen had planned every detail to make it perfect. She worked in a supermarket for five hours every Saturday morning, a tiring job particularly at this time of year. She worked the cash register and sat in a cold, windy part of the shop where the doors were always opening and the December wind came biting around her shoulders. They didn't like her wearing a jacket, so she wore three vests and a small jumper under her nylon coat. She looked much fatter than she did at school, where she was the secretary in a nice sensible wool dress. The school had central heating and nobody leaving doors open. Jen saved the supermarket money to make it a great Christmas for them all. She bought crackers and table decorations, she bought mincemeat for the pies, she got the kind of tin of biscuits they would never have dreamed of buying normally, she had a tin of chestnut purée and a box of crystallised fruits.

Jen wasn't a great cook, but she had planned their Christmas lunch so often that she felt she could now do it in her sleep. She even knew what time she should start the bread sauce. It would be the first *real* Christmas Day for Martin and Stevie, she reminded herself. The lovely Tina had never been very strong on home cooking, and she liked to spend the festive season drinking to people's health in wine bars or restaurants and clubs.

Jen felt a wave of unease, as she often did about Tina. She hoped there was no danger of Tina spoiling their first Christmas by arriving suddenly and being sweet. Tina being sweet was sickening. Martin seemed to forget how she had humiliated him so often and so publicly. How other men had been found sipping wine and eating dainty delicate sandwiches when Martin got home tired from work. In the days when Stevie was a toddler and well out of the way in his playpen and a wet nappy, Martin could barely remember the number of times when Tina had disappeared, overseas, sometimes for weeks on end, or how her working hours in the casino seemed to stretch to mid-morning and Martin had been unable to go to work until she returned.

Tina had been able to think of Stevie alone in the house; Martin had not.

But nowadays, when Tina was so charming and undemanding, it seemed that he could no longer remember the bad old days. Tina was so unfairly good-looking: long legs, long fair hair, and whatever she wore looked marvellous. She looked girlish and in many ways too young and irresponsible to be Stevie's mother. Jen, on the other hand, looked matronly, she told herself sadly, and as if she were the mother of many older children. Life was unfair, Jen was the same age as the leggy Tina, twenty-nine. Next year they would both be thirty, but one of them would never look it, not even when she turned forty in ten years' time.

Jen pinned up the Christmas cards, attaching them to ribbons and trailing them across the wall.

'That's nice,' Stevie said approvingly. 'We never had that before.'

'What way did you put them then?'

'I don't think we put them at all. Well, last year Dad and I were in a hotel, remember, before you came along, and before that I don't think Mum had much time.'

He was neither wistful nor critical. He was just seeing things the way they were.

Jen seethed to herself. Mum had no time, indeed! Mum who had no real job, who just played about in that casino, had no time to put up Christmas decorations for her husband and little son. But plain old Jen had time, boring Jen who worked in a school from nine to four. Industrious Jen who dragged herself and Tina's son on two buses so that the boy could see his mother with minimum fuss. *And* took the money out of her own purse to pay for the taxi in order to keep the peace. But nobody ever said Jen hadn't got time to do anything. There was no mercy, no quarter given second time around.

Martin approved of the decorated house; he went round touching the sprays of holly and ivy over the pictures, the candle in the window, the tree that was waiting for them all to fill.

'This is lovely,' he said. 'It's like a house you see on telly, not like a real house at all.'

It was meant as high praise. Jen felt a strange stinging in her eyes. It was a hell of a lot more real, she thought, than when bloody Tina was here with her high-flying friends and her idiotic chat and no time to make a Christmas for anyone.

Well, at least this year, like last, Tina would be miles away on a cruise ship dealing the cards, calling the numbers and looking divine for the passengers. That's what she had done last year, just before the divorce was final. Jen had gone home to her mother, who had warned her all through the five days of Christmas that it wouldn't be easy to marry a divorced man and raise his child. Martin said it had been a lonely Christmas in the hotel, though Stevie had enjoyed the organised games. They had both thought it was better not to spring too much on him at once, let him have a Christmas alone with his father to show him there was some stability in a changing world. He had only been seven, poor little fellow. Still, he had adapted very well, all in all. He certainly didn't think of her as a wicked stepmother, and he didn't cry for his golden-haired mum. Jen just wished they wouldn't think of her as so ordinary and of Tina as something special and outside normal rules.

She had lit a fire for them and they sat, all three of them, around it talking. For once nobody asked what was on the television, Martin didn't say he had to go out to his workshed, Stevie didn't say he wanted to go to his room. Jen wondered why she had felt so uneasy about Tina and their Christmas. It was childish to have these forebodings. She laughed at the other school secretary who read her star sign carefully before taking any action each morning; people would laugh too at Jen with her premonitions and funny feelings that something was going to happen.

'Tina rang me at work today,' Martin said just then.

Martin hated being rung at work, he was on the counter in a busy bank, he hated being called away from his window. Only the greatest of emergencies would make Jen pick up the phone to call him. Surely it must have been the same with Tina, and this must have been an emergency.

'Her cruise has been cancelled apparently so she's not going abroad. Only told them at the last minute, and no money or anything. Very unfair of the company.' Martin shook his head at such sharp practice.

'So Mum will be at home at Christmas?' Stevie was pleased. 'Will I go over to see her in the morning or what?'

Jen found that her eyes were tingling for the second time that evening. Damn her. Damn Tina for ever. Why couldn't she be ordinary? Why couldn't she have found a man and lived with him and married him like ordinary people did? Why did it have to be this flapper life of cruises and casinos and clubs? And Lord, if it had to be that, why did it have to be this shipping company of all of them that had to fail? There had to be a reason. Now they would have to disrupt their nice Christmas Day, just so that Tina could see her son for a couple of hours. A son she couldn't care about or why would she have given him away? It was so unfair. Martin was shaking his head doubtfully.

'That's the problem,' he said, looking from one to the other. 'You see, she had all her plans made to go abroad and she has nobody, nobody at all for Christmas. She doesn't think she could stay in her house all alone. She doesn't like the idea of being all alone for Christmas.'

'Lots of people are alone for Christmas,' Jen said suddenly before she had time to think.

'Yes, well sure they are. But this is Stevie's mum. And you know Tina, she likes to have a thousand people round her, but they all think she's going away.'

Jen stood up pretending to fix the curtains which didn't need to be touched at all. They didn't seem to notice her.

'So what will Mum do then if she doesn't want to be alone? Will she go away somewhere else?' Stevie wanted to know.

'I think she will, she said she was ringing round a bit,' Martin said. Of course she was ringing round a bit, but who better to ring first than the kind ex-husband. Just to make him miserable and guilty, just to make him offer her Christmas Day with her son, with a nice meal cooked for her. Yes, obviously Tina would ring Martin first, the old reliable, always there. No matter if she ran away, she knew he'd take her back. Until he met Jen and found that life could be lived on a normal level.

It had taken Jen to open Martin's eyes to Tina and her way of going on. But, Jen thought grimly, she mightn't have opened them enough. It was hovering in the air between them. *The invitation.* It had to come from Jen, but she was not going to issue it. No, she was most definitely not. She would pretend that she hadn't understood the tension.

'Then I won't be able to see her on Christmas Day?' Stevie said.

Jen was bright. 'If she had been on the cruise you wouldn't have seen her anyway, remember?' she said. 'And you've given her your Christmas present and hers to you is under the tree.'

'But if she has nowhere to go ...?' Stevie said.

'Oh Stevie, your mum has a thousand places to go, you heard your father say just a second ago she has a thousand friends around her.'

'I said, she likes a thousand friends – it's a different thing.'

Jen knew what she would like to do at that minute. She would like to have put her coat on and walked out in the rain and wind. She would like to have hailed the first taxi she saw and gone to Tina's house. Then she would have taken Tina by the neck and shaken her until there was only a flicker of life left in her body. Briskly she would get back into the taxi and come home to inquire if anyone would like drinking chocolate as a treat.

But Jen wouldn't do this because it was not a civilised thing to do. It would be considered the act of a madwoman. In England, that is. In the more hot-blooded Mediterranean countries it would be totally understood. But this was not a country of Latin lovers and passionate jealousy, this was a civilised place. So Jen fixed a slightly dim smile to her face, as if she were talking to a very senile man and a very young baby instead of her husband and stepson.

'Well, no point in us bothering about all that now, is there? Your mum is well able to sort out her own problems, Stevie. Would anyone like some drinking chocolate?'

Nobody felt like any, so Jen stood up deliberately and made some for herself. She knew if she had put three mugs on the tray they would all have had it, but why should she? Why should she play nanny to them both? While they stared into the changing pictures of the fire and worried about beautiful Tina and her troubled Christmas.

When Stevie had gone to bed, Jen talked about the super-market. They wanted her to work Saturday, Sunday, and the two days before Christmas. Should she do it? It was a lot of money, in the middle of January they would be sorry if she hadn't done it. On the other hand, maybe it was just tiring herself out for the sake of a wage packet. Might they be happier if she were to stay at home a bit and relax? She wondered what Martin thought.

'Whichever you like best,' he said. His face still looked pre-occupied to her. Suddenly it was all too much effort. Suddenly the mask of civilised behaviour fell right down to the ground.

'Whichever I *like*?' she said in disbelief. 'Are you actually mad, Martin? Whichever I *like*? Do you think anyone in the whole world would *like* to get out of a nice warm bed and leave a gorgeous man like you still in the bed, get dressed, flog over there and deal with bad-tempered customers, watch that people don't nick things at the till, see women with big rings on spend-ing hundreds of pounds a time on food? If you think anyone would choose to do that, you must be insane.' He looked at her, dumbfounded. Jen had never spoken to him like this before. Her eyes were blazing and her face was contorted with anger.

'But why did you ... I mean, I thought you wanted to earn ... you never said ...' He was stammering, unable to cope with the woman in the other chair who had turned into a stranger.

'I wanted to have extra money to make this a nice home

for you and Stevie and me, that's what I wanted. And I never allowed myself to think about the sum of money that goes from your salary every month towards Tina's mortgage. Not even on a Saturday afternoon when I look at her house, which is bigger and better than our house, do I question the fact that you pay towards its upkeep when we all know that sometimes Tina earns three times what you and I earn together. I know, I know her work is uncertain. Some weeks she might earn nothing. I know, but isn't she lucky, my, my, my, what a bit of luck that we never suggested that she should get a regular job like the rest of the world has to do?' Jen paused for breath and pulled away her hand which Martin was reaching for. 'No, let me finish, perhaps I should have said it before, perhaps I am the guilty one for pretending it doesn't matter, for putting on a brave little face, but that's what I thought you needed. You'd had enough tempers and tantrums with the last one, I thought you needed a bit of peace and calm around you now.'

'But I need *you*, *you're* what I want,' he said simply.

She went on, nodding her head in agreement. 'Well, that's what I tried to be, calm, and putting a good face on things, and I suppose that's what I'll go on doing. It was just when you asked me to suit myself or whatever you said – "whichever I like" – as if there was any question. Of course I'd like to be at home here, getting up late, pottering around a bit, maybe doing the plants and sort of just enjoying ourselves, like people do. Like some people do.'

'But I thought you found it a bit dull here, and that's why you like to run off and be with people, meet them, and have a bit of money as independence, you know.' His big honest face looked at her, bewildered. No wonder Tina had walked over this kind, uncomplicated man.

Jen opened the kitchen cupboard and showed him the store of luxury foods, the crackers, the table decorations. She gestured to the bright, shining ornaments and the electric lights on the Christmas tree. She wordlessly touched the new standard lamp that stood up by his chair, the curtains on their smart new rail, the brass box that held the logs for the fire. 'This is hardly spending money just for me to fritter away. I got these things for our house. I don't hoard my salary for me any more than you do with yours. I spend it making a nice home for us all, and I'm sorry, Martin, I do *not* want to have Tina here to wreck our first Christmas, I really don't, and that's why I'm so upset. I just want you and me and Stevie and a bit of time. Time to talk. Is that so awful?'

'Tina? Come here for Christmas? There was never any question of that!'

'Oh yes, there was. I saw it in your eyes, you wanted brave Jen, nice calm Jen to say Let's be civilised, let's ask Stevie's mother to share our groaning board. Well, I won't and that's that.'

'But you can't think I want Tina here, can you? After all the Christmases she ruined on me and on Stevie, after all the heartbreak and the lies and the deceit. Why would I want her here again? I am divorced from her remember, I'm married to you. It's *you* I love.'

'Yes, but what about Tina's Christmas?'

'Oh, she'll find somewhere, don't worry.'

'I'm not worried. It was you who sounded worried when you were talking earlier. With Stevie, you definitely looked upset about her.'

'I was and I am a bit, you see I didn't finish while Stevie was there.'

'What was it?' Jen was anxious.

'Oh, just Tina upsetting people. As well as the Christmas fiasco, she has plans to go abroad in the New Year. More or less permanent job, she says. We had a talk about the house, her house. She won't need any more help towards it, she's going to let it apparently, and she said she's sending us something to recompense me.'

'I'll believe it when I see it.'

'Yes, well, so will I but the main thing is no more monthly cheque to her.'

'Are you upset because she's going?'

'Only for Stevie. I was thinking that he will miss her, but then tonight when I came home to this lovely place I think he'll only miss her for a little while, he's got such a good home here. You've made it for both of us a real home.'

But she wouldn't give in completely, she had come out in the open and she wasn't going to put on her gentle Jen mask again immediately.

'So what was the upset about if you're not going to miss Tina, and you think Stevie'll get over it? Why were you so depressed?'

'I was thinking that I might be a very dull sort of husband. Tina ran away from me, you ran off to work at weekends, I thought it was because I was dull.' He looked so sad, she knelt down in front of him.

'I thought I was dull too, I wanted to be tigerish like Tina, but I never thought you were dull for a moment, not for one second. I swear it.'

He kissed her in the firelight.

'Men are very silly really,' he said. 'We never think of saying the obvious. You are beautiful and fascinating and I've always been afraid since the first time we met that you might be too bright for me, and think I was a dreary sort of bank clerk encumbered with a son. I couldn't believe it when you wanted to take us both on. I never think of Tina except in relief that she gave me Stevie and that it turned out as it did. It never crossed my mind to compare you. Never.'

'I know.' She soothed him now, he seemed so worried. But he was struggling to find words. He was determined to pay her the compliment that was in his head and his heart but he had never been able to say.

'Years ago,' Martin said, 'they used to have mainly black-and-white films and when one was in colour they used to say "In Glorious Technicolor …" That's what you're like, Glorious Technicolor to me.'

He stroked Jen's mouse-brown hair, and her pale cheek, he put his arms around her and hugged her to him in her grey cardigan and her grey and lilac skirt. He kissed her lips that had only a little lipstick left, and closed her eyelids that had no make-up, and kissed her on each of them.

'Glorious Technicolor,' he said again.

Pulling Together

Penny wrote an airmail letter to her friend Maggie in Australia every week. Every week she wrote about life in the staff room, how Miss Hall had become like a caricature of a schoolmarm, how the children were now *all* delinquents instead of just a steady thirty per cent of them. She wrote about the parents, some of them filled with mad hopes and belief that their daughters were going to conquer the world. It was a hard thing to live in a land that seemed to have been ruled for ever by a woman monarch and had had a woman prime minister, Penny wrote, it gave girls notions that they could get anywhere. That was nearly as bad as the old notions, the notions that they could get nowhere.

She wrote about the time passing so quickly that it was quite impossible to believe she was facing her fifth Christmas in this school. If anyone had told her that when she started. If anyone had said that at twenty-seven Penny would have had one job, and one job only, in a girls' school in a city miles from her home. In a small, shabby flat that she had never done up because she had never intended to stay in it. She wrote to Maggie about cold autumn evenings where she stood, hands deep in her pockets, cheering on the hockey team because it showed a bit of school spirit and pleased the games mistress, how she helped at the school play because it was solidarity and how, even now, without a note in her head she would help for the fifth time to organise the carol concert.

She didn't need to tell Maggie *why* she did all these things. Maggie knew. And Maggie was a good friend, she never mentioned it. Not once, not even in the middle of her own airmail letters about teaching in the bush, about having killed a kangaroo and thinking everyone would be furious but in fact they had congratulated her; about how the school seemed to empty at sheep-shearing time, about Pete the fellow she had a De Facto with. De Facto meant a real proper live-in relationship, it counted if you wanted to become an Australian citizen.

Maggie never enquired why Penny didn't leave if it was all so wearying. Maggie knew about Jack. And she knew enough about Jack not to ask any questions about him. In the first days of the romance Penny had written flowingly about him, about the way Jack had come into her life, suddenly and surely. Knowing that he loved her, knowing that he needed her. Jack had been so sure of everything, Penny felt foolish in her doubts. Doubts about his being married for one thing, about his not leaving home, about his wanting to keep it all quiet.

Jack loved everything about Penny that was funny, he said. Funny, lively and free. She was so different from the predictable women who all came up with the same self-centred line over and over ... Penny felt that this line had something to do with wondering when, if ever, the man would be free. So that was a road which she had never gone down in the early days. She had sworn to him that she, too, wanted to be free, she couldn't bear the idea of being tied down, she couldn't change her horses in midstream now, she couldn't suddenly, when she passed her quarter-of-the-century mark, tell this man that she wanted a little security. She had picked up Germaine Greer's book *The Female Eunuch* and read again the chapter which said that there is no such thing as security. She willed herself to believe it, and refused to read any articles suggesting that Germaine Greer herself might have had a change of heart.

Because of Jack's position and the fact that he and his wife had to go out to a lot of functions, even though it was all meaningless, of course, and the smiles they had for the cameras were phoney and empty ... Penny could tell nobody about their relationship, about how he came to the little flat whatever evenings he could steal and how she had to be there most of the time just in case, and not complain on the many evenings that he had *not* been able to steal time. She had hinted a little of that to Maggie at the start, but Maggie, secure in her De Facto, had been too kind to pursue it. Maggie had simply said that if you loved someone you did, and that was it. You took the package. You couldn't break down the kit and reassemble it, much as *she* would like to reassemble Pete without his insatiable thirst for ice-cold beer! It had been heartening, and Penny hugged the notion to herself when things were bleak, which was more and more of the time.

There had been three years of Christmas Days of loving Jack, and now a fourth was coming. They had been the saddest days of her life. Sitting watching gleeful television shows, telephoning her mother and stepfather miles and miles away, assuring them she was happy and thanking them for all the gifts. Fingering whatever scent bottle Jack had given her, and waiting all the time until he could steal the minutes. Last year he had only come for a quarter of an hour. He had pretended he needed to pick something up from his office, he said. The children had insisted on coming, he had left them in the park to play. He couldn't stay.

She had cried for two hours after he had gone. She had put on her dark raincoat and walked past his house later in the afternoon. It was full of lights and Christmas trees and cards on the wall, and mistletoe on the light. Who was that for? The children were too young. But don't ask him. Never let him know that she had seen it.

It had been so very lonely that this year she had decided to go away. To somewhere where there was sunshine, and preferably no Christmas. Morocco she had thought of, or Tunisia. Somewhere Muslim and warm. But Jack had been appalled. Hurt and even a little shocked.

'You must think very little of me, and how I have to go through this charade if you just run away,' he had said. 'We could all do that … run away from things. I thought you loved me and that you would be here. Have I ever failed to come and see you at Christmas? Answer me that.'

Penny realised it had indeed been selfish of her. But now that it was the season of fuss and school hysteria, now that the shops had been playing Christmas songs for weeks already and her eyes felt tired from looking at so many pictures of domestic bliss, Penny wished that she had been firmer, wished that she had told Jack in level tones without any catch in her voice that going away for eight days did not mean an end to the love that had consumed her for almost four years and would continue to be the centre of her being for ever. She should have been strong enough, and found the words that didn't make it look like a gesture, a hurt little reaction … Something from the

I-can-stand-on-my-own-feet brigade. But now it was too late. He was going to take her to supper on Christmas Eve, in a new place, very simple, no one he knew or his wife knew would go there. It sounded like a cafe from what he said, Penny thought glumly. She could imagine herself having sausage and beans and a nice cup of milky tea.

Still, it was better than … She stopped and racked her brains to think what it was better than. She looked over at Miss Hall, fifty-five possibly, same old jumper and skirt for years and years, same old shabby briefcase, sitting tucked away in a corner reading her newspapers, face grey, hair grey, outlook grey. Yes, it was much better than being Miss Hall, with her big house that must have been worth a fortune in the square and her lack of interest in anything except being left alone with her precious papers. Penny often wondered what, if anything, she ever read in them, she seemed to have no interest in current affairs, in politicians or in gossip columns. She had not been seen doing crosswords.

There was a knock on the staff-room door, it was Lassie Clark. Lassie was one of the pupils that Penny liked least, a big sulky-looking girl with hair deliberately arranged so that it covered most of her face. She had a way of shrugging her disapproval and boredom without even seeming to move her shoulders. Without bothering to move the curtain of hair that hid her eyes and mouth, Lassie muttered that she had been told to report here at three-thirty.

'What was it for this time?' Penny asked. Lassie was one of the familiar faces reporting because of essays not done, excuses not given in by parents, homework unfinished.

'Don't know,' Lassie said. 'Something about an old school pageant, I think. Or else it was something else.'

Penny longed to give her a good hard smack. She must remember to tell Maggie in her next letter that teaching in an all-girls' school, working in an all-female staff room, was definitely not natural. It made you mad, sooner rather than later. And in Penny's case, now.

She controlled her urge to attack the girl.

'How old are you, Lassie?' she inquired, her voice over-pleasant.

Lassie looked out from the mane of hair suspiciously, as if this were a trick question.

'What do you mean?' she asked.

'Come on now, it's not one of the hard ones.'

'I'm fifteen,' Lassie admitted without any pleasure.

'Good, well by that age *I'm* sure you know what you were asked to report here about, was it the bloody pageant or was it some other damned thing. Say which it was and don't have us all here all night.'

Lassie looked up in genuine alarm. The teacher seemed to have lost control.

'It was the bloody pageant,' she said with spirit, knowing she could hardly be corrected about the word since the teacher had used it first.

'Well, what did you do? Not go to rehearsal?'

'Yeah.'

'What a fool you are! What a stupid, foolish girl who can't see further than her own foolish face. Why didn't you go to the rehearsal and get shut of it? Now you have to stay in and spend a half an hour in the classroom writing for no reason, and they'll be looking out for you tomorrow, and they'll probably insist you dress up as a shepherd or an angel or something. Why the hell couldn't you have just gone along with it and stood there like the rest of us have to year after bloody year just because it's easier?'

Penny had never seen Lassie's eyes before – they were quite alert, interested and frightened at the same time.

'I suppose so,' she said grudgingly.

'You can be sure of it. Right, come on, it's my day to take all the rebels, the burning young women protesting against the system.'

'What?' Lassie asked, confused.

'Forget it. I'm as bad as you are. I'll see you down in the hall.'

She went back into the staff room to collect her books and saw Miss Hall. The older woman was looking out of the window at the wet branches.

'Sorry for that outburst,' Penny said.

'I didn't hear you. What happened?'

'Oh, I shouted at Lassie Clark,' Penny explained.

'I wonder why her parents had a child if they wanted a dog,' Miss Hall said unexpectedly.

'Perhaps she made it up herself as a name.'

'No, she was always called that, for the last nine years anyway. I remember when she was in Juniors thinking how silly it was.'

Penny was surprised. Miss Hall wasn't noted for remembering anything about the children.

'Lord, but she's a troublesome child anyway, no matter what she's called,' Penny said. Her voice was down and unlike her normal cheer.

'It's just Christmas,' said Miss Hall. 'It brings everyone down. If I had my way I'd abolish it totally.'

Penny, who had been feeling precisely the same way, didn't think she could agree.

'Oh, come now, Miss Hall, it's lovely for the children,' she said.

'It's not lovely for people like Lassie,' Miss Hall said.

'Nothing would please *her*, spring, summer, autumn or winter.'

'I think Christmas is particularly hard, we have such high expectations, and it never lives up to them.'

'You sound like Scrooge,' Penny said with a smile to take the criticism out of her voice.

'No, it's true, whoever felt as happy on Boxing Day as on Christmas Eve? Child or adult.'

'That's too gloomy.'

'What about you, you're a cheerful little soul. Since you came here you have always been able to see the bright side, even when there *is* no bright side. But isn't it true what I say? You will have a happier day before Christmas looking forward, than after it looking back.'

Penny had never had a conversation like this with the crabbed Miss Hall before. Definitely Christmas brought out if not the best in people, at least something different.

'Funnily enough, in my case Boxing Day will be better, because then Christmas will be over and I won't have to sit on my own worrying and waiting for it to be over. But I do take your point for other people.'

Miss Hall's eyes rested on her, and she thought she saw tears in them.

Penny had been so brave for years that she bristled at the thought of pity or even a hint of sympathy. 'No, no, I don't want you to feel sorry for me,' she said hastily.

'I don't have time to feel sorry for you, Penny, I feel so sorry for myself there isn't room for anyone else in my sympathy.'

The older woman looked so wretched that Penny, with her hand on the door and about to leave to supervise those girls who had been kept in after school, paused.

'Is there anything I could do ...?' She was hesitant. Miss Hall was always so sharp and caustic. Even now, having admitted she felt miserable, she would surely somehow turn against any warmth that might be offered to her.

But Miss Hall looked not her usual confident self, she looked as if she were teetering on the brink of saying something, of giving a confidence.

'No ... thank you ... you are very kind to ask. But it's not something anything can be done about really.'

'Something can be done about everything,' Penny said with false cheer, as if she were talking to a child.

'Then why can't you do something about *your* Christmas and make it a day to be happy about instead of sitting wishing it was over?' The old teacher spoke with concern, not with malice. There was no way the question sounded offensive.

'I suppose because, in my case, there are things I don't *want* to change. And I have to take what goes with my having made this choice.'

'Yes, that's reasonable, if you know it's something you can cure by choice, then I agree you're right in saying that something can be done about everything.' Miss Hall nodded, as if pleased to have teased out the logic of the thing.

'And in your case?' Penny felt very bold, as if treading on dangerous ground.

'It's not a matter of simple choice, there's something I should have done years ago, or rather not done years ago. But let's leave me for a moment. That poor sulky child, Lassie, I don't suppose she has much choice.'

'She could make herself a bit more pleasant,' Penny complained.

'Yes, but it's not going to affect her Christmas. Pleasant or unpleasant it will still be the same.'

'How do you know?' Miss Hall had never been heard to speak a word about the children, as if they had no lives outside the school wall.

'Oh, the usual way, through the gossip. Her parents are divorcing, her mother is already pregnant by the new chap, her father has already moved into a flat with his girlfriend. The last thing any of them want for the festive season is the big gloomy face of the child they called Lassie lurking around them.'

'So what's she going to do?'

'What can she do? Demand as much attention in each place as she can, make them all feel miserable and guilty. That looks like the form. No amount of being charming is going to bring about what she really wants, which is her old home back again as it was. Solid and safe.'

There was such sympathy in Miss Hall's voice, such understanding. Penny dared to speak again of personal things . . .

'I am on my own at Christmas, as I told you. If there's any way I could come and see you or meet you . . . or . . .' She couldn't ask the woman to her flat in case she would be there when Jack found his stolen half-hour. He would be speechless with rage to find an old schoolmarm on the premises. But at least she could offer to go to the old woman's huge terraced house later in the evening, when Jack had gone back to what she considered the bosom of his family and what he described as an empty charade which he had to stay in for the sake of the children until they were old enough to understand.

'No, no, you are very kind.'

'You *said* that already. Why not? *Why* can't I come?' Penny sounded bad-tempered now.

'Because I won't be there. My house is no longer mine. It has had to be sold.'

'I don't believe you. Where are you living now?'

'In a hostel.'

'Miss Hall – is this a joke?'

'It would be a very unfunny one if it were.'

'But why? That was your home for ages I heard, your father and grandfather lived there. Why was it sold?'

'To pay my debts. I'm a gambler, a compulsive gambler. I would like to say I *was* a gambler, but like alcoholism, we must always use the present tense.'

'You can't live in a hostel ... for ever.'

'I may not have to. When the sale of the house is completed I shall probably have enough to get myself something small.'

'But how terrible for you. I had no idea.'

'No, nobody has any idea, nobody except my group ... you know, the support group, and of course the people I owe money to, they know only too well. It would be disastrous if at this stage the school were to know. I don't think the Head would extend a great deal of seasonal charity and understanding, I'd much prefer if she weren't to find out.'

'No, no, of course,' Penny gasped.

'There can always be some cover story about my selling the house and the pictures, and all the lovely furniture because it was too big for me, too much to manage.'

'Was it horses or cards, Miss Hall?'

Miss Hall smiled. 'Why do you ask?'

'I suppose it's all so unlikely, and I wanted to keep the

conversation sort of down to earth rather than getting upset on your behalf.'

Miss Hall approved of this. She gave a wry sort of smile.

'Well, to make it even more unlikely still, let me tell you it was chemin de fer.'

'In a club?'

'Yes, in a plush club an hour's journey from here by train. Where nobody knows my name. Now you've heard everything.'

Penny realised that she must leave. This minute. There were no parting shots. No sympathetic reassurances. Just close the door behind her.

In the hall, sitting sulkily at her desk, was Lassie. Alone.

'Leave it and go home,' Penny said.

'I can't, I *have* to do it. You said yourself it was silly not to have gone to the thing, I'd better not be done twice.'

'True. I just thought you might like to get home.'

'No point really, no one there,' Lassie said.

'Like me,' Penny said with a grin.

'Yeah, but you chose it, and you're old.'

'No, I didn't choose it, and I'm not old.'

'Sorry.' Lassie managed a half-smile.

'Get on with it then, I'll just think something out.'

Penny sat in the big classroom they used as a detention hall. In front of her Lassie Clark struggled with a page and a half of essay, 'Changes in the Neighbourhood,' which nobody would read once it was written. Its only function was to be a punishment.

Penny thought about her mother and stepfather and how it was too late now to come home to them for Christmas even if she wanted to, which she didn't. It would startle them, it would bring back too many memories of the house when Daddy was alive, when she had been a little girl, when there were no problems ahead.

It was too late to go on the trip to a country where there would be no Christmas, only swimming pools and palm trees and buffets in the sun.

But it would not be too late to rescue Christmas if she *chose* to. If she *chose* to open up some of the windows in her heart that Jack had made her close. That she had closed out of blind love for him that was not real love, it was infatuation and fear of losing him.

She thought it all through, slowly, clearly, and without emotion. It would suit them all, but there would be problems, of course, foolish not to face the problems.

There must be no aura of pity about it. No hint of the Last Chance Saloon. If Penny were going to do it, she would spend not one minute of her time trying to keep the peace between the gruff and distant Miss Hall and the sulky, resentful Lassie. She took a deep breath and looked at the child sitting at the desk in front of her. Was it her imagination or had she actually pushed her hair behind her ears? Her face looked if not alert, at least responsive.

'Lassie,' she said.

'Have you thought it all out?' Lassie asked.

'Yes, and I'm going to offer you something. A lot depends on what you say, so listen to me until I've finished.'

'All right,' Lassie said agreeably.

She listened and there was a silence.

'Do you have a nice big flat?' she asked.

'No, it's *not* very nice, I never did much with it, I never thought I'd stay there long, you see. But there is room. A spare room with a sofa bed for Miss Hall, you could bring a sleeping bag and have the sitting room and the telly if you turn it down low. I have my own room.'

'There's ten days before Christmas,' Lassie said impassively.

'Yes. So what?' Penny didn't know whether to be pleased or annoyed that the child was taking it all so matter-of-factly. To be invited to stay with two teachers for Christmas was surely not something that came your way every day.

'I meant we could get it looking nice, paint it up a bit maybe, put up a tree, practise cooking. I don't suppose any of us are much use at that.'

'No.' Penny couldn't hide a smile.

'Will she have any money?' Lassie cocked her head towards the staff room.

'No, I don't imagine so, but I have enough. Nothing luxurious.'

'They'll probably give me some money, I can bring that, I mean they'll be so glad to get rid of me.'

'You can't live with me *for ever*, you know, Lassie, just Christmas.'

'That's all right, that's all we'll need each other for,' Lassie said.

'I'll go and tell Miss Hall. I'm sure she'll agree.'

'She'll be mad if she doesn't,' Lassie said sagely.

Miss Hall listened impassively. Penny began to wonder was the world filled with people who took everything very lightly.

'Yes,' she said eventually, 'that would be very nice. I'm glad you told her about my predicament, after all, I told you about hers. So *we're* all right. *You're* the only problem.'

'What do you mean I am the problem?' Penny was so indignant, she could hardly speak. Here she was offering these two misfits a home for Christmas and now suddenly *she* was defined as the one with the problem.

'Well, it must be a man, a married man,' said Miss Hall without any condemnation in her tone. 'And since you haven't had time to discuss this new arrangement for Christmas with him, is there not a possibility that you may regret your invitation to us, or that he'll resent it, or that it will seem somehow the wrong thing to have done?' Miss Hall asked as mildly as she might have asked were there more biscuits with morning coffee.

'No. No, there is no possibility of that. None whatsoever,' Penny said.

'And you mustn't take this kind of thing on every year, dear.' Miss Hall was solicitous. 'You are such a good warm girl, it would be easy to find yourself taking on lame ducks instead of taking on someone undamaged to love them and to be loved back.'

It was said softly and with great warmth, and yet Penny knew she must respond in practical brisk tones.

'You *are* good to say that.' She smiled. 'And of course you're right, it's just a one-off, just this Christmas, after that we'll all be cured and ready to get on with whatever there is to get on with.'

She would have plenty to write to Maggie about, and little to say to Jack. Because Jack would know it was no empty gesture, no seeking his attention. Just a sign that she was indeed cured and well on the way to recovery.

A Hundred Milligrams

If you stayed with Helen's mother until Easter, she'd still complain that you were leaving too early after Christmas. So this year they decided to be firm. They would arrive on the Sunday night and they would leave on Thursday. Four nights under her mother's roof and almost four full days. This year, their tenth Christmas together in Mother's house, they would avoid all the pitfalls of other years. They would list them in advance.

There was the cold. Mother's house was freezing. So they would give her a gas heater, one you could buy cylinders for, then she couldn't complain that it was eating electricity or running away with fuel bills since they would provide the cylinders. They would wear warm clothes and take two hot-water bottles each. They would never shiver in public nor would they spend any time at all trying to persuade her to get central heating.

Then there was the matter of drink. They would just provide their own bar up in the bedroom, cunningly disguised as part of their luggage. They would need many more drinks than Mother's sideboard would offer, and they would have to take them in private. Mother was a great one for spotting broken veins, shaking hands, signs of liver damage where none existed. Then there was Mother's advice. They would listen to it with blank, polite faces. This year they would not rise to the bait, this year they would not be drawn into an argument they couldn't win. They would say to themselves and each other as soon as they woke, the tips of their noses freezing in that igloo of a bedroom ... they would say, 'Mother is not technically very old. But Mother has always had the mind of an old woman. She will not change so we must change and not allow ourselves to be hurt by her.' They would chant that at each other. Then surely it couldn't be too bad.

And indeed it wasn't too bad. This tenth Christmas was a lot better than the ones that had gone before. The house was warmer for one thing, and they had invited neighbours in for sherry and mince pies at intervals. That cut down on the amount of time left for Helen's mother to shake her head sadly and say she didn't know what the world was coming to, and that values had all changed and not for the better.

It was Thursday morning. Today they were going to leave. They had planned to take Mother out to lunch. The boot of the car would be packed already. They would drop her home after the meal in the hotel and they would fly off home, guilty but free, and this year congratulating themselves on having kept the peace.

Helen leaned over and gave Nick a kiss. He reached for her but she leapt smartly out of bed. That was another thing that you couldn't do in Mother's house. It felt wrong, you had the notion she could come in the door at any time. Anyway there was plenty of time for all that back home.

'I'll make us a cup of tea instead,' she said.

'All right,' Nick grumbled.

Her mother was in the kitchen. 'Wouldn't you think he'd get up and get you a cup of tea?' There was a hard, thin line of discontent. Helen reminded herself to watch it, she must not allow herself to become defensive, she must let no note of anything mutinous into her voice.

'Oh, we take it in turns,' she said lightly.

'A lot else he has to do. Any man in his position should be glad to make you tea and take it up to you – honoured to be allowed to make you tea.'

'Look, while I'm here why don't you go back to bed too and I'll bring you a cup.'

'No, I'm up now. I might as well stay up. It's back to normal for me now that you have to go. I thought you were going to stay till the New Year at least, and Miss O'Connor was saying that she was surprised ...'

'Yes, she has a great capacity for being surprised, I've noticed that,' said Helen, banging out the cups and saucers. Then she remembered. Only five more hours. Be nice, be calm. Nobody except us gets hurt in the end.

'Did she have a nice Christmas herself, Miss O'Connor I mean?' she asked in staccato tones.

'I've no idea. She goes to a sister. It's all she has.'

The kettle was taking an age to boil.

'Does he lie in bed all day at home now? Does he get dressed at all?'

Calm, Helen. Slow. Fix on the smile. 'Oh, we usually get up about the same time, you know. One day I make the breakfast, the next day he does. Then we take Hitchcock for a walk and I get the bus; Nick gets a paper and goes home.' Her voice was bright and sunny, as if she were telling a tale of an ideal lifestyle.

'And has he turned his hand to cooking even?'

'Oh yes indeed. Well, you saw over Christmas how much he likes to be involved with everything.'

'He only carried plates in and out, from what I could see.'

The kettle must have two holes in the bottom of it, no container ever took three hours to boil. Helen smiled on and fussed with a tray.

'Trays, is it? There used to be a time when two mugs of tea did fine in the morning.'

'You have such nice things here, it's a pity not to use them.'

'I suppose he can't wait to get his hands on them altogether. I saw the way he was admiring that cabinet. Fetch a good price, he said.'

'I think Nick was trying to reassure you, Mother, you said that you had no possessions, no antiques. Nick was pointing out to you that you do have nice pieces of furniture.'

'He's in a poor position to point anything out, a man who did what he did. I wouldn't thank him for pointing things out to me.'

'That would be a pity, Mother.' There was steel in her voice. Helen knew she was on the thinnest ice yet. Usually it had been hint and innuendo. Now it was being said straight out.

'No I mean it, Helen, to humiliate you and me. To make us the object of pity here. Don't think that everyone doesn't know. Everyone knows. It's only because I have always been on my own, always had to bear the burden, that I'm able to do it again.'

'I don't think it's a humiliation for me or for you that Nick is redundant. All over the country people are being laid off work. The one it's worst for is Nick, and we're lucky that we have something coming in. And that we don't have five children like some of his colleagues have.'

'Well, that's another thing. Ten years married and no children, just a dog with a ridiculous name, Hitchcock. Who would call a dog a name like that?'

'We thought it was a nice name, and we love him. And we don't inflict him on you, now do we? He's in a kennel, looking out, waiting for us.'

Wrong. Wrong. She shouldn't have said that. It showed an eagerness to be away. Too late to try to retrieve it. Was that actually a sound out of the kettle, did it intend to boil after all?

'I don't know how you put up with it, Helen, you who had everything. I really don't know how you take it all, instead of having some spirit.'

'If I could get Nick a good job in the morning there's no one who'd be more delighted than myself.' She had the smile of a simpleton on her face now, willing her mother to drop the conversation, to go no further down the path where she was leading.

'I don't mean just about the job. I mean about the other thing,' her mother said. And now it was said, it had to be acknowledged.

'Yes?' Polite, interested, but giving nothing away.

'Don't yes me, Helen, you know what I mean. The woman. Nick's woman.'

'Oh yes, well, that's all over now.' Still light, no evidence of the heavy lump of putty gathering in her chest.

'What do you mean, it's over? It's not like Christmas that it's here and then it's gone. It's not simple like that.'

'It is really, Mother, that's exactly what it is.'

'But how can you let him away with it? How can you bear him with you after … after all that?'

'Nick and I are very happy, we love each other, that was just something that happened. It was a pity that people got to know about it but they did.'

The kettle had boiled. She warmed the teapot.

'And you go on as if nothing has happened, after all that.'

'What is the alternative, Mother? Just tell me. What else would you like me to have done? What would you have liked, Mother, if I had asked you?'

'I'd like for it never to have happened.'

'So would I, so would I, and I think so would Nick and so would Virginia. But it did happen.'

'Was that her name, Virginia?'

'Yes, that's her name.'

'Well, well. Virginia.'

'But tell me, Mother. I'm interested now, what would you like me to have done? Left him? Got a restraining order? Tried to get an annulment? What?'

'Don't raise your voice at me. I'm only your mother who wants the best for you.'

'If you want the best for me, then stop torturing me.' Helen's eyes filled with tears. She went upstairs with the tray of tea. 'I've blown it,' she sobbed to Nick, 'on the last bloody morning I've blown it.'

He laid her head on his shoulder and patted her until the sobs ceased.

'Let's put some brandy in our tea,' he said, 'and get back under the covers before you become a relic of the Ice Age.'

It would have been nice if nobody had known about Virginia. Helen knew. She had known from the start, but she had said nothing. She thought that it would not last. Virginia was young and pretty and silly and worked in Nick's office. That kind of thing happened all the time, very very rarely did it break up people's marriages. If the wife was sensible and kept her head. Only confrontations were dangerous, and why make a perfectly decent, honourable man like Nick be forced to choose between his practical wife, Helen, and the pretty little Virginia? Why not take no notice and hope that Virginia found some other man? That is precisely what would have happened and was about to happen, and it would all be past history if it hadn't been for the accident.

It was two Christmases ago and there was Nick's office party. Helen had begged him not to take the car. The place would be full of taxis. Why have the responsibility? They had argued good-naturedly about it at breakfast. They worked out milligrams, how many would make you drunk. They agreed that they could both drive a car perfectly after four times the permitted amount, but that some people couldn't so that was why the rules had to be so strict and the limit made so absurdly low. He had promised that if they all got really bad, he would leave the car there and sneak in for it the next morning. Helen knew that his romance with Virginia was coming to an end, she had been happier then than for a long time before.

She realised that Nick wasn't staying out so late, there were fewer furtive phone calls. She congratulated herself on having weathered the storm.

At seven o'clock Virginia had telephoned her very drunk and tearful. Virginia had asked her to be especially nice to Nick over Christmas because Nick was a wonderful person, a really wonderful person, and would need a lot of consolation. Helen agreed, grimly thinking that the only thing worse than being sober and receiving a telephone call from a drunk was to be the wife receiving a telephone call from the mistress. The combination of the two was heady stuff.

A little later Nick had phoned saying he hoped that some of the girls hadn't phoned her saying anything silly. Helen said it was all incomprehensible but please don't drive home. Nick said he had to take this silly girl home, she was making a fool of herself. He hung up before Helen could beseech him to get a taxi.

Nick had told her later that the drive was something he would remember for the rest of his life. The drive rather than the accident.

The streets seemed to be full of tension and danger, the lights of every car were hostile, there were drivers peering through windscreens in the rain, there were unseasonable hootings, and abuse was hurled in a most unfestive manner.

Beside him Virginia, who had been sick, was sobbing and clutching at his arm. She hadn't meant to telephone Helen, but it came over her that Helen should be informed. Earlier that day she had told Nick she was going away for Christmas with someone else. Now she seemed full of regrets and second thoughts, she wanted reassurance that she had done the right thing at every turn. Nick was concentrating hard on the road and didn't answer, she pulled his arm and the car swerved into the left lane right into the path of a big truck.

Virginia lost two teeth, broke her shoulder, and cracked two ribs. Nick lost his driving licence for three years, the firm lost the car, but since it also lost Nick and most of his colleagues some months later that wasn't very important. The case went on and on, and insurance companies provided more and more explanations on each side, and Virginia gave an interview to a paper about how her chances of matrimony might well be lessened by her facial injuries and referred to having a fling with a married man in her office, a married man who had managed to destroy her life completely. Somewhere in the world there is always someone who sees things in papers and brings them to the attention of other people, and somewhere there was somebody who managed to send it to Mother's friend Miss O'Connor, with the name of the firm and the coincidence of the accident and everything they thought Helen's mother should know.

For two years she had managed not to speak aloud about it, only making allusions. But this morning it had come out. And Helen hadn't been ready. 'I'm sorry,' she snuffled into her brandy-flavoured tea. 'You've been so marvellous, and now I've thrown it all away. She'll sulk during lunch, and it's all been wasted.'

Nick warmed his ice-cold hands on the nice cup of tea and brandy and stared ahead of him. Downstairs they could hear Helen's mother banging the furniture about a bit. It was a message as clear as any drumbeat in a jungle, a message that she was annoyed and upset and that things would not be easy when they got up.

'If only we didn't have to come here. Just one Christmas, the two of us on our own with Hitchcock,' Helen said wistfully.

Nick's eyes seemed misty, she thought, or was the early morning's brandy making her feel a bit dizzy?

'I wonder how many milligrams there are in this tea?' she asked. More to cheer him up than anything else. He turned and looked at her. She had been right, there were tears in his eyes.

'Remember that plate you broke here years and years ago?' he said.

She was surprised. 'Yes, the one that Mother made such a fuss about.'

'Well, we mended it, remember, you held bits of the plate with eyebrow tweezers and I painted on the glue.'

'And you couldn't see the cracks in the end.' She wondered why he was thinking of this, it had happened years ago, just another occasion when her mother had behaved badly and Nick had smoothed it out.

'But when it was done she wanted to use it at once and we had to say no and put it high, high up so that it would have time to harden. It looked all right but it wasn't really. You couldn't use it. Touch it and it would all fall apart.'

'Yes, we put it in one of those little plate stands?' There was a question in her voice. What was he talking about?

'If anyone came into the room and looked at that plate, they'd have said to themselves that it was a perfectly sound plate, they'd have no reason to think otherwise. But it wouldn't have been. Not until the glue hardened. It was fine in the end, of course, but for a long time it was only pretending to be a real plate.'

'Well, yes.'

'It's a bit the same here, isn't it? We've been pretending to be real plates in front of your mother. We won't let her see any of the cracks or the glue or anything. We've been putting on such a brave face for her. We've not stopped to ask ourselves is it real or is it not?' He had rarely sounded so serious.

'Yes, I suppose it was a way to go. We could have endless discussions and analyses, and what happened and why, and where did we go wrong, but I don't know. Would it have made things much better?'

'It might have been more honest. You might have wanted to throw me out but couldn't, not with us having to put on an act all the time for your mother, pretend that this was the successful lovey-dovey marriage of the century.'

'Well, it's been a pretty good marriage most of the time, hasn't it?' Helen said.

'Is that you talking or is it you talking for your mother's ears?'

'It's me talking, do you not think the same?'

'I do, but I'm the villain, the cheat, the partner without a job, the drunk driver, I'm in no position to make definitions.'

'Oh Nick, don't be so ridiculous, what's over is over. I said that ages ago.'

'No, you've got too used to pretending, you're being too tolerant ...'

'Listen to me.' Her face flashed with anger. 'When my mother attacks you I feel a sense of loyalty to you so strong it almost sweeps me away, when she says one word against you I become so fiercely protective you would never believe it. Perhaps she has done some good for us in that way, because her every attempt to drive us apart only glues us together.'

'Is it real glue, is it good firm glue, do you think, or are we only pretending to get along fine?'

'I don't know how you test these things. We could go downstairs and fling the plate on the floor, for example, and if it broke we could say, "Boo hoo the plate wasn't properly stuck together."'

He looked very pleased. 'In a way your bad-tempered old mother has a lot to be thanked for. She stopped us making any decision before the glue had hardened. It has hardened, hasn't it, Helen?'

There was an almighty banging downstairs. The noise had increased in case it wasn't being heard. Nick and Helen got up and tore the linen off the bed they wouldn't have to sleep in that night. They heaved the furniture round the room for pure divilment and realised that for them there would be nothing gained by examining the cracks and pulling them to see if they would come apart. Other people might want to talk it to death, but they knew the face they had shown the difficult woman downstairs was a real face, and they only had four more hours of putting slightly phoney smiles on it. The kinds of smiles a million other people were putting on their faces like children's masks over Christmas.

The Christmas Baramundi

She had met him first at the fish market on Christmas Eve. It was very early in the morning, but already crowded. Their hands touched as they each pointed to the same ocean perch.

'That one,' they said at the same time.

They all laughed, Janet the schoolteacher, Liam the banker, and Hano the younger son of the fish merchant.

'You have it,' Liam said gallantly.

'No, no, you were the first,' Janet countered.

Hano said, 'He has many brothers and sisters, you can have one each.'

'I don't like to think of his brothers and sisters,' Janet said.

'I know, but we're very hypocritical, aren't we?' Liam had a crinkly smile that lit up his face.

'Who was it said they could never eat anything that had a face?' Janet looked thoughtfully at the slabs of fish, each one with a very definite face, some of them indeed with expressions that you could almost define.

'Hey, you'll have us eating bread and cheese for Christmas,' he said.

Janet sighed. 'No, that's the problem, point out all the disadvantages about something and then go ahead and do it all the same.'

'Mine's different, I favour the ostrich technique; pretend things don't have faces, or brothers or sisters. Just grill them and eat them.'

'Poach them surely, or cook them in foil. This is much too big to grill.' Janet took things literally.

'Have coffee with me,' Liam said suddenly.

Hano wrapped their fish for them. Janet paid in cash, Liam used a gold credit card. He took her by the elbow and they went across the way to the little cafe where people drank small cups of coffee and ate delicious Italian bread. Hano waved them goodbye. He would love to have gone with them, to have talked and laughed as they did so easily. Instead he would have his father's eye on him and his uncles' and the eyes of his two older brothers. This was one of the busiest days of the year. He should be working, reaching out towards customers, not dreaming.

More and more people bought fish for Christmas Day. Going to the market in Pyremont was now almost a tradition. The customers enjoyed the experience as much as the fish they bought. Look at that couple, for example: the man was rich, he had a jacket that Hano would have to work for five years to earn. His watch was gold. He didn't even look at the receipt he signed. He surely didn't *need* to come here and buy fish; someone could have got it for him. Perhaps he was lonely; maybe he had a row with his wife. Possibly he was a bachelor or a divorced man. He must be about thirty-five or forty.

Janet was asking herself all these questions, too, as they went together for coffee.

But by the time they were sipping their espresso and eating

the warm foccacia she didn't care if he was married or single, if he had twenty people waiting at home for him or nobody. He was just so easy to talk to. They sat on high stools and talked about Christmas Eve in other lands. Liam had been in New York some years, always a wet, cold day. He remembered coming out of his office and trying to join the throngs getting last-minute gifts in stores where a million others had the same idea. They took such short vacations in New York City. Not like here in Sydney, where the world closed down for weeks.

'Well, it is our summer holidays,' Janet said, a trifle defensively. She was always apologising for the long school vacations that teachers enjoyed. Her other friends said her life was a holiday. But their lives weren't filled with shrill young voices, clamouring young personalities, and the need to be on stage from the moment the first bell rang to the last. Of course, she had never wanted to be anything else but a teacher, she told Liam, and she told him about a Christmas she had spent in France that was meant to improve her French but actually had only improved her interest in wine.

And then they talked about wines they both liked, and around them people wandered around the fish counters and water gushed through the drains and lumps of ice that hadn't yet melted fell to the ground. They talked, Liam and Janet, with the excitement of people getting to know each other and afraid to ask the question that might nip it all before it got started. Each was buying a fish large enough to feed a family. Neither wore a ring, but that meant nothing. They each noticed that the other was in no hurry to go home, but again that might have no significance. When their third set of empty coffee cups was taken away they could pretend no longer.

'I suppose I'll have the shakes if I drink any more,' Liam said.

'Me too.' Janet looked glum suddenly.

'What's wrong?' he asked.

'I wish sometimes that I could get out of that schoolgirl habit of saying *me too*, and *me first*. It's the only downside of working with children; you start talking like them.'

'Do you have children?' His question was sudden and direct.

'About two hundred and eleven at last count,' she said, and then as if trying to make up for being flippant, added, 'but I say goodbye to them each day at four o'clock.'

'I see.' He seemed pleased.

'And you?' She hoped her voice sounded light.

'About ninety at last count, but that's only in the bank,' he said. And she knew that he left them behind when he left the bank too.

'I see.' She was very pleased. She might have to fight a woman for him, but no adorable little toddlers who needed their daddy.

They had been there for a long time.

'Would you like to meet again?' he asked simply.

'Yes please,' she said. It was a jokey thing to say. It hid her eagerness, her great relief. Would he ask for her phone number? Would he give her his? When would he suggest? Janet felt the breath almost choke her.

'So what do you suggest?' he asked. He was leaving the decision to her.

'I think saying *same place, same time, next year* is a bit on the long finger.' She looked at him with her head on one side, waiting. Janet hated women who behaved like this, but she felt she had to. It was the only alternative to letting him see the eager longing in her face to see him again, to get to know him better.

'Oh, I hope to know you very well by this time next year,' he said softly. 'Very well indeed.'

Janet felt herself shiver. It was the kind of shiver that her mother said meant someone was walking over your grave.

'Well then,' he said. 'Well then.' He suggested a restaurant, he suggested lunchtime three days later.

'Will they be open?' Janet asked. She didn't want to risk their missing each other.

'Oh yes, they'll be open.'

They looked at each other as if there was still something more to be said. He picked up a brochure advertising all the different kinds of fish that were on sale and tore a piece off. It had a picture of a baramundi. He quickly wrote some figures.

'In case you change your mind,' he said.

She tore another baramundi off and wrote her number.

'In case you change yours,' she said.

'No, it's the highlight,' he said, with a mock bow of his head.

'I look forward to it,' Janet said, and skipping the puddles of water made from the hosing of the fish stands, she made her way to her car. She turned around to look back once, and he was still standing there. She wondered why they hadn't wished each other Happy Christmas. Everyone else was saying that to people that they had only just met. Perhaps it was because they each believed the other had something to do at Christmas, something to unpick or sort out.

Janet shared a house with three other teachers. They each had a large sunny room that acted as their own bed-sitting room. They had a huge shared kitchen and two bathrooms. They had a small garden with four sunbeds placed around it. Everyone said they were mad to rent this expensive property. They could each have found a deposit and a mortgage for a house of their own, but at this point none of them wanted that. And they got on very well together for women in their twenties and thirties. They didn't live each other's lives. They paid a woman to come in once a week to clean, nobody kept their television up too high, and if lovers were invited into people's rooms, it was not discussed, nor was anything untoward ever audible. They always laughed about their living arrangement, calling it Menopause Manor. But they could do that because it was far from the truth.

This year none of them had gone away for Christmas. They would eat together in their garden. There were various reasons. Janet had a new stepmother; she wanted to give the woman a breathing space before descending on her for holiday festivities. Maggie had a married lover who was not available for Christmas Day. Kate was writing her thesis and had decided to give it three solid weeks of six hours a day in Menopause Manor. Sheila was from Ireland; sometimes she flew the whole way back there, but this year she had not saved the money and couldn't find the enthusiasm for rain and sleet, so she too was staying in Sydney. It would be a happy, undemanding day for the four of them. They would be unsentimental, probably a little tipsy. They would not mention Maggie's man, and the futility of it all; they would not make Sheila sad about the Emerald Isle by singing 'Danny Boy'; they would be supportive about Kate's MA thesis; and they wouldn't know that Janet had just met the most marvellous man in the whole world, so they could have no attitudes about it.

On Christmas Eve, Janet sat out in the garden; the night was warm and smelled of flowers. She could hear the sea in the distance. She wondered where he was at this moment, the man called Liam with the crinkly smile, who said he was in banking. He had not said he worked in a bank; that was a subtle difference. It was ten o'clock. The telephone rang. Although she felt sure it must be from Ireland for Sheila, Janet went to answer the call.

'Janet?'

'Liam?' she said immediately.

'Just thought I'd wish you Happy Christmas. We forgot to do that today.'

'So we did. Happy Christmas,' and although she hated waiting, she managed not to say any more.

'Have you still got the baramundi?' he asked.

'Yes, yes indeed.' Another pause.

'Have a happy day,' he said.

'You too.'

They hung up. Janet went back to the garden and hugged her knee as she looked up at the starlit sky. She knew exactly why she had been so unforthcoming. She wanted to be allowed to dream over this Christmas. She wanted to think of Liam and his smile, and the fact that he had been thinking of her at ten o'clock on Christmas Eve night. She did *not* want to hear about his wife and children if they existed, or his longtime live-in lover who understood him, or his messy divorce. She wanted to think of him as a man who was looking forward to seeing her in three days' time. A man who could talk about anything and who understood everything. A man who said that this time next year they would surely know each other very well.

She sat and hugged her secret to herself. She had not been in love for six years. Not since she was twenty-two. Since then there had been people, but nothing that counted as real love. She had forgotten how utterly wonderful it felt; how silly and feathery and quite unconnected with the real world. She heard bells ring and she knew there must be church services. She heard merrymakers calling goodnight down the street. It was Christmas Day.

There was no breeze, but still she shivered. That was the second time today. For no reason Janet remembered her mother helping to zip her into her first formal dress on her eighteenth birthday.

'I'm so happy,' Janet had said, looking delightedly at her reflection in the mirror.

'You'll never be as happy as you are now this minute,' her mother had said. Janet had been furious. Her mother had taken all the gold and glitter away from the moment. And she had never forgotten it, even though her mother had been wrong.

Janet had been happier than on her eighteenth birthday. When she was twenty-one she had fallen in love with Mark and been happy for fourteen months, every day and night. Why did she have to remember her mother's words now, the words of a woman who was never truly happy, who always saw the bleak side? Too much laughter meant tears before bedtime, too much good weather meant headaches later on, people being nice and warm and welcoming meant that sooner or later they would prove to have feet of clay.

Janet's mother had been dead for four years. Her father had married again; a different kind of woman, small and round and giggling. Janet couldn't understand what they saw in each other, but that was not remotely important. Maybe they found what she and Liam had found, however unlikely it seemed. After all, her father had met Lilian at a television studio where they were both members of a studio audience, and now they were married. Janet had met Liam at the fish market this morning, and he had told her that this time next year they would know each other very well indeed. He had just telephoned to wish her Happy Christmas. The good times were only starting.

On Christmas Day the others said that Janet must have had some attitude-changing substance. She had a funny, happy smile all day. Janet made the salads, set the table in the garden, baked the potatoes, and chilled the wine. Not the most domesticated of the four in the household, she insisted on doing it all this time. She cooked the ocean perch lovingly. This was a fish that Liam had touched with his own hand. This was a fish they had laughed over, a fish that brought them together.

The day seemed curiously long; happy but long. Janet thought that it must be seven o'clock when it was still only five o'clock. Somehow the days passed. And then it was the morning. The morning of the lunch. Janet realised that she had shadows under her eyes because she had slept so poorly. She was placing far too much hope on this, too much importance, reading more into it than there was. Very probably, but it still didn't make her sleep. There was no hairdresser open so she shampooed her hair and spent hours trying to get it into the kind of shape she wanted. She had planned to wear her peach-coloured shirt and a grey denim skirt, but she thought it made her look as if she had stepped from the chorus of *Oklahoma!* It was too hot for a jacket, too smart a place for a beach dress. Janet had been wearing jeans when she met him at the fish market. She wanted him to know she had other clothes.

By the time she had settled on a linen skirt and plain white T-shirt, it was time to call the taxi. The taxi was late. Janet was red-faced and anxious when she arrived at the restaurant.

'I ordered us oysters,' he said, his eyes anxious to know if he had done the right thing.

Normally Janet hated the pushy male thing of ordering for the little woman. But he was trying to be generous, to make a gesture. She smiled such a smile, her face nearly broke in half.

'What could be better?' she asked.

The lunch was like their coffee break at the fish market only better. They talked about the world of banking and how hard it was for Liam to meet real people any more. Instead he met corporate people and committees and read reports and acted on them. And Janet told him eagerly about school and how there was no time to get to know the children and find out what they really wanted to do, and what they were like and what they hoped for. Instead you had to follow a curriculum, and get them to pass exams, and achieve a good result for the school.

They couldn't finish the prawns, the sauce was too rich. As they pushed them around their plate he said unexpectedly, 'Will you spend the afternoon with me?'

'Yes, of course, where?' she asked.

'I have a place.'

Her smile was broad again. He couldn't be married or tied up or have a whole complicated lifestyle that he was cheating on. Not if he said he had a place.

'Oh, really?' Janet said, face full of hope and eagerness.

'Well yes, I booked, just in case, just in case you'd say yes,' he said.

It was a motel. A place you book. He had been so sure of her, he had thought it worthwhile to make a reservation. Her heart felt heavy, and her face must have shown it.

'Something's wrong,' Liam said.

'No, not at all.' Her smile was brave and his came back. He was so simple, really, and straightforward. He had liked her, liked her enough to invite her to lunch, to call her on Christmas Eve, to order oysters, to book a place for the afternoon, to be with her. Perhaps *she* was the selfish one, she was the one demanding commitment, assurances that he was available, and a catch, and maybe even a meal ticket. She was a liberated woman. Janet knew you could meet and enjoy each other as equals if you wanted to. The days of demanding that a man be a protector or a provider were long gone.

'So shall we stop pretending to eat these prawns?' he asked with a laugh.

'I've given up the struggle,' she agreed.

They drove to the motel. A place Janet had often passed and wondered idly how it made a living. Now she knew; they rented by the hour. It was clean and functional. He had a bottle of wine in a cool bag that he had brought with him, another sign that he had known she would agree to the motel, and he poured her a glass. It was a good wine from a vineyard they had talked about, but today it tasted like vinegar. He was a gentle and courteous lover, and he lay afterwards with his arm around her shoulder, protectively, as if they had often lain like this before and would for many more years. Her heart lifted for a while. Perhaps this is the way people were nowadays. Behaviour had changed. You didn't have to play games, pretend to be hard to get, exchange sexual favours for continued attention, trade sex for commitment.

'I got you a little gift, a silly thing,' he said, and he reached out for a wrapped parcel that he had on the bedside table. She couldn't have loved him more. She was glad that she hadn't played at being outraged when he suggested an afternoon in a motel.

'What is it?'

No present she had got this Christmas could compare. It

was a little tin fish, the kind of thing you might hang on a Christmas tree or, if it had a magnet, it could be stuck to the refrigerator door.

'It's a baramundi,' he said, pleased with what he saw as her pleasure. 'To remind you of when we met pointing at that fish and fighting over it, and then becoming friends.' His arm was around her again, squeezing tightly.

'Great, great friends,' he said, appreciatively. She turned over the little fish in her hand.

'It's great,' she said. She knew her voice was flat, her pleasure was not real.

'Well, it's a jokey gift,' he said, embarrassed.

'No, it's great.' She wanted to be a million miles from here. Why had she not taken her car? She tried to remember. It had something to do with being available for him. Well, she had been that all right. In spades. Now she would have to ask him to drive her to somewhere near her home or to a taxi rank. It would be squalid. But she would not let it be that way. If only she could guard herself, not say anything foolish.

'Where does your wife think you are?' Janet heard herself ask.

He looked as if she had hit him, but he rallied.

'She didn't ask. I didn't say.'

'And your children?'

Why was she asking these things, ruining what was good between them.

'They're in the pool. They don't know where I am. I work such long hours they don't expect me to be around.'

He had answered her truthfully. He had asked her nothing in return.

They left the bed where they had been so happy, so close, and she noticed he took a very long time having a shower. As if he had been to a sports club or a gym. He passed her a clean towel when she went into the shower, and she held it for a long time to her face to force away the tears that she thought might come.

In the car he was still boyish and happy. But he was so intelligent, surely he must know that whatever they had was over? He asked where she lived and she suggested that he leave her in Balmain.

'No, no, door-to-door service,' he laughed, then looking at her face, realised it might be crass. He patted her on the knee.

'I didn't mean to be flip. It was lovely,' he said.

'Yes indeed.' She tried, but she couldn't put any life into her words.

He drove her to the gate. Out in the back garden Maggie might have been half sleeping in the sun, dreaming of her married man who could not leave his family at this festive time. Kate would be in her room studying. Sheila might have gone to play tennis and beat back the guilt about not having gone home to Ireland for Christmas Day. None of them would know that Janet's heart had cracked in two.

Liam was looking at her.

'Will we meet again?' he asked; his face was enthusiastic. He liked talking to her, laughing with her, holding her, making love with her. He couldn't see any reason why it could not go on, as sunnily and easily as it had begun.

Struggling to be fair, Janet couldn't see any reason either, except that she knew it was over.

'No, but thank you, thank you all the same,' she said.

He looked at her sadly.

'Was it the fish? Was it the little Christmas baramundi?' he asked anxiously.

'Why do you say that?' Janet asked.

His face was troubled.

'I thought you'd like it. I thought it was silly and sentimental and not commercial. I could have got you a pin, a brooch or something for five hundred dollars, but I thought it looked wrong somehow.'

'The fish is great,' Janet said.

'And we did meet over a baramundi,' he said.

'Or something,' Janet said.

There was a silence. Liam looked at the house.

'It's a nice place to live,' he said, as if trying to bequeath her a good life.

'Oh yes, it is.' She realised he didn't know. He had never asked if she lived with a man, a husband, or children. He just assumed she was a free spirit who could live life in compartments as he could.

'Has it a garden at the back?' They talked like strangers now, like people at a cocktail party.

'Yes, a small garden. Do you know, Liam, I was happier there on Christmas Eve than I ever was in my life, and than I ever will be again.' She knew her voice was very intense and that he was looking at her uneasily. But somehow it was a great relief to have something defined. They said that women became more like their mothers as they grew older.

Janet shivered. She felt that she was becoming very like her mother. Soon her face would tighten into a hard smile. What a pity there was nobody she could talk to about it. The man who was saying goodbye at her gate was someone who might have understood, had things been different.

This Year It Will Be Different

Ethel wondered had it anything to do with her name. Apart from Ethel Merman there didn't seem to be many racy Ethels; she didn't know any Ethels who took charge of their own lives.

At school there had been two other Ethels. One was a nun in the Third World, which was a choice, of course, but not a racy choice. The other was a grey sort of person, she had been grey as a teenager and she was even greyer in her forties. She worked as a minder to a Selfish Personality. She described the work as Girl Friday; it was, in fact, Dogsbody, which scanned perfectly, and after all, words mean what you want them to mean.

These were no role models, Ethel told herself. But anyway, even if it weren't a question of having a meek name, a woman couldn't change overnight. Only in movies did a happily married mother of three suddenly call a family conference and say that this year she was tired of the whole thing, weary of coming home after work and cleaning the house and buying the Christmas decorations and putting them up, buying the Christmas cards, writing them and posting them so that they would keep the few friends they had.

Only in a film would Ethel say that she had had it up to here with Christmas countdowns, and timing the brandy butter, and the chestnut stuffing, and the bacon rolls, and bracing herself for the cry 'No sausages?' when a groaning platter of turkey and trimmings was hauled in from the kitchen.

She who had once loved cooking, who had delighted in her family's looking up at her hopefully waiting to be fed, now loathed the thought of what the rest of the world seemed to regard as the whole meaning of Christmas.

But there would be no big scene. What was the point of ruining everyone else's Christmas by a lecture on how selfish they all were? Ethel had a very strong sense of justice. If her husband never did a hand's turn in the kitchen, then some of the blame was surely Ethel's. From the very beginning she should have expected that he would share the meal preparation with her, assumed it, stood smiling, waiting for him to help. But twenty-five years ago women didn't do that. Young women whooshed their young husbands back to the fire and the evening newspaper. They were all mini-Superwomen then. It wasn't fair to move the goalposts in middle age.

Any more than it was fair to stage a protest against her two sons and daughter. From the start those children had been told that the first priority was their studies. Their mother had always cleared away the meal after supper to leave them space and time to do their homework, or their university essays, or their computer practice. When other women had got a dishwasher, Ethel had said the family should have a word processor. Why should she complain now?

And everyone envied her having two strong, handsome sons

around the house, living with her from choice. Other people's twenty-three- and twenty-two-year-olds were mad keen to leave home. Other women with a nineteen-year-old daughter said they were demented with pleas about living in a bed-sitter, a commune, a squat. Ethel was considered lucky, and she agreed with this. She was the first to say she had got more than her fair share of good fortune.

Until this year. This year she felt she was put-upon. If she saw one more picture of a forty-seven-year-old woman smiling at her out of a magazine with the body of an eighteen-year-old, gleaming skin, fifty-six white, even teeth, and shiny hair, Ethel was going to go after her with a carving knife.

This year, for the first time, she did not look forward to Christmas. This year she had made the calculation: the thought, the work, the worry, the bone-aching tiredness on one side of the scales; the pleasure of the family on the other. They didn't even begin to balance. With a heavy heart she realised that it wasn't worth it.

She didn't do anything dramatic. She didn't do anything at all. She bought no tree, she mended no fairy lights, she sent six cards to people who really needed cards. There was no excited talking about weights of turkey and length of time cooking the ham as in other years. There were no lists, no excursions for late-night shopping. She came home after work, made the supper, cleared it away, washed up and sat down and looked at the television.

Eventually they noticed.

'When are you getting the tree, Ethel?' her husband asked her good-naturedly.

'The tree?' She looked at him blankly, as if it were a strange Scandinavian custom that hadn't hit Ireland.

He frowned. 'Sean will get the tree this year,' he said, looking thunderously at his elder son.

'Are the mince pies done yet?' Brian asked her.

She smiled at him dreamily.

'Done?' she asked.

'Made, like, cooked. You know in tins, like always.' He was confused.

'I'm sure the shops are full of them, all right,' she said.

Ethel's husband shook his head warningly at Brian, the younger son.

The subject was dropped.

Next day Theresa said to the others that there was no turkey in the freezer, nor had one been ordered. And Ethel turned up the television so that she wouldn't hear the family conference that she knew was going on in the kitchen.

They came to her very formally. They reminded her of a trade-union delegation walking up the steps to arbitration. Or like people delivering a letter of protest at an embassy.

'This year it's going to be different, Ethel.' Her husband's voice was gruff at the awkward, unfamiliar words. 'We realise that we haven't been doing our fair share. No, don't deny it, we have all discussed it and this year you'll find that it will be different.'

'We'll do all the washing-up after Christmas dinner,' Sean said. 'And clear away all the wrapping paper,' added Brian. 'And I'll ice the cake when you've made it. I mean after the almond icing,' Theresa said.

She looked at them all, one by one, with a pleasant smile, as she always had.

'That would be very nice,' she said. She spoke somehow remotely. She knew they wanted more. They wanted her to leap up there and then and put on a pinny, crying that now she knew they would each do one chore, then she would work like a demon to catch up. Buzz, buzz, fuss, fuss. But she didn't have the energy, she wished they would stop talking about it.

Her husband patted her hand.

'Not just words, you know, Ethel. We have very concrete plans and it will begin before Christmas. Actually it will begin tomorrow. So don't come into the kitchen for a bit, we want to finalise our discussions.'

They all trooped back to the kitchen again. She lay back in her chair. She hadn't wanted to punish them, to withhold affection, to sulk her way into getting a bit more help. It was no carefully planned victory, no cunning ploy.

She could hear them murmuring and planning; she could hear their voices getting excited and them shushing each other. They were trying so hard to make up for the years of not noticing. Yes, that is all it was. Simply not noticing how hard she worked.

It just hadn't dawned on them how unequal was the situation where five adults left this house in the morning to go out to work and one adult kept the house running as well.

Of course, she could always give up her job and be a full-time wife and mother. But that seemed a foolish thing to do now, at this stage, when the next stage would be the empty nest that people talked about. They were all saving for deposits, so they didn't really give her much, and they were her own children. You couldn't ask them for real board and lodging, could you?

No, no, it was her own fault that they hadn't seen how hard she worked and how tired she was. Or hadn't seen until now. She listened happily to the conversation in the kitchen. Well, now they knew, God bless them. Perhaps it hadn't been a bad thing at all to be a bit listless, even though it hadn't come from within, it wasn't an act she had put on.

Next morning they asked her what time she'd be home from work.

'Well, like every day, around half-past six,' she said.

'Could you make it half-past seven?' they asked.

She could indeed, she could have a nice drink with her friend Maire from work. Maire, who said that she was like a mat for that family to walk on. It would be deeply satisfying to tell Maire that she couldn't go home since the family were doing all the pre-Christmas preparations for her.

'You could always go to the supermarket,' Theresa said.

'Am I to do any shopping?' Ethel was flustered. She had thought they were seeing to all that.

She saw the boys frown at Theresa.

'Or do whatever you like, I mean,' Theresa said.

'You won't forget foil, will you?' Ethel said anxiously. If they were going to do all this baking, it would be awful if they ran out of things.

'Foil?' They looked at her blankly.

'Maybe I'll come back early and give you a bit of a hand . . .'

There was a chorus of disagreement.

Nobody wanted that. No, no she was to stay out. It was four days before Christmas, this would be a Christmas like no other, wait and see, but she couldn't be at home.

They all went off to work or college.

She noticed that the new regime hadn't involved clearing away their breakfast things, but Ethel told herself it would be curmudgeonly to complain about clearing away five cups and saucers and plates and cornflake bowls and washing them and drying them. She wanted to leave the kitchen perfect for them and all they were going to do.

She wondered that they hadn't taken out the cookery books. She would leave them in a conspicuous place, together with all those cookery articles she had cut from the paper and clipped together with a big clothes-peg. But she must stop fussing, she'd be late for work.

Maire was delighted with the invitation to a drink after work. 'What happened? Did they all fly off to the Bahamas without you or something?' she asked.

Ethel laughed; that was just Maire's way, making little of the married state.

She hugged her secret to herself. Her family who were going to do everything. Things were exciting at the office, they were all going to get new office furniture in the new year, the old stuff was being sold off at ridiculous prices. Ethel wondered would Sean like the computer table, or would Brian like the small desk. Nothing would be too good for them this year. But then, did second-hand goods look shabby, as if you didn't care?

With the unaccustomed buzz of two hot whiskeys to light her home, Ethel came up the path and let herself in the door.

'I'm back,' she called. 'May I come into the kitchen?'

They were standing there, sheepish and eager. Her heart was full for them. While she had been out drinking whiskey with lemon and cloves in it, stretching her legs and talking about the new office layout with Maire, they had been slaving. Poor Maire had to go back to her empty flat, while lucky Ethel had this family who had promised her that things would be different this year. She felt a prickling around her nose and eyes and hoped that she wasn't going to cry.

She never remembered them giving her a treat or a surprise.

This is what made this one all the better. For her birthday it had been a couple of notes folded over, from her husband, a request to buy herself something nice. Cards from the children. Not every year. And for Christmas they clubbed together to get her something that the house needed. Last year it had been an electric can opener. The year before it had been lagging for the cylinder.

How could she have known that they would change?

They looked at her, all of them waiting for her reaction. They wanted her to love it, whatever they had done.

She hoped they had found the candied peel – it was in one of those cartons without much identification on it, but even if they hadn't she'd say nothing.

She looked around the kitchen. There was no sign of anything baked or blended or stirred or mixed or prepared.

And still they looked at her, eager and full of anticipation.

She followed their eyes. A large and awkward-looking television set took up the only shelf of work space that had any length or breadth in it.

An indoor aerial rose from it perilously, meaning that the shelves behind it couldn't be got at.

They stood back so that she could view the full splendour of it.

Sean turned it on with a flourish, like a ringmaster at a circus. 'Da-daaaaa!' he cried.

'I *told* you this Christmas was going to be different to the others.' Ethel's husband beamed at her.

From now on she could look at television as well as the rest of them; she'd be as informed and catch up on things and not be left out, just because she had to be in the kitchen.

All around her they stood, a circle of goodwill waiting to share in her delight. From very far away she heard their voices. Sean had known a fellow who did up televisions, Dad had given the money, Brian had gone to collect it in someone's van. Theresa had bought the plug and put it on herself.

Years of hiding her disappointment stood to Ethel at this moment. The muscles of her face sprang into action. The mouth into an ooooh of delight, the eyes into surprise and excitement; the hands even clasped themselves automatically.

With the practised steps of a dancer she made the movements that they expected. Her hand went out like an automaton to stroke the hideous, misshapen television that took up most of her kitchen.

As they went back to wait for her to make the supper, happy that they had bought her the gift that would change everything, Ethel got to work in the kitchen.

She had taken off her coat and put on her pinny. She edged around the large television set and mentally rearranged every shelf and bit of storage that she had.

She felt curiously apart from everything, and in her head she kept hearing their voices saying that this Christmas was going to be different.

They were right, it felt different; but surely it couldn't be on account of this crass gift, a sign that they wanted her forever chained to the kitchen cooking for them and cleaning up after them.

As she pricked the sausages and peeled the potatoes it became clear to her. They had done something for her for the very first time – not something she wanted, but something; and why? Because she had sulked. Ethel hadn't intended to sulk, but that's exactly what it had been. What other women had been doing for years. Women who had pouted and complained, and demanded to be appreciated. By refusing to begin the preparations for Christmas, she had drawn a response from them.

Now, what more could be done?

She turned on the crackling, snowy television and looked at it with interest. It was the beginning. She would have to go slowly, of course. A lifetime of being a drudge could not be turned around instantly. If, as a worm, she was seen to turn too much, it might be thought to be her nerves, her time of life, a case for a nice chat with some kind, white-coated person prescribing tranquillisers. No instant withdrawal of services. It would be done very slowly.

She looked at them all settled inside around the flat-screen television, satisfied that the Right Thing had been done, and that supper would be ready soon. They had no idea just how different things were indeed going to be from now on.

Affair Before Christmas

Judith realised very suddenly that her husband was having an affair. And in a very public place. It was as she was bending over a cabinet of chilled foods in the supermarket three weeks before Christmas; she looked up to ask Ken whether he would prefer the lemon mousse or the raspberry flavour and she caught a look on his face that she had never seen before. He was biting his lip and looking at her as if he wished more than anything that things had not turned out like this. As if he was almost unbearably sorry.

She didn't suspect, she just knew. Suddenly everything moved slightly as a jigsaw might if it had been juddered out of place, or as a camera focuses. Suddenly everything made sense.

She got such a shock that she dropped the package into the big food compartment and gave a little gasp. He looked at her with even greater concern.

'What is it?' His eyes were kind and worried.

'It's nothing, just a cramp.' She straightened herself up and held her side as if she had a stitch. 'Put that lemon mousse in the trolley for me like a love. I'll just go and sit down for a moment. Can you finish the list?'

He helped her to a chair and all the time his hand on her arm felt like the painful grip of someone who was taking you into custody.

Judith told herself to stay calm. Calm, calm. Say nothing now, she must think. She would *not* burst into tears in the supermarket in front of people who knew her from every Wednesday evening. She would not accuse Ken of betraying her to the interested audience of a weary after-work crowd of shoppers. She would have to think it out carefully.

They were playing 'Silent Night' from the speakers around the store. There were holly and tinsel chains everywhere.

'I won't let it happen until after Christmas,' Judith said to herself. She actually articulated the words. 'It will not be said until Christmas is over. I deserve that and the children deserve it. He cannot break up our lives until we have had our Christmas.'

Every Wednesday they came to do their weekly shop. Judith had made it into a great outing for the family. First they filled the trolley; she was in charge of expensive items like special desserts as a treat, and all the cleaning materials, since nobody else knew what was running out. Tommy and Jane bought the fruit and vegetables. They weighed them out carefully. Judith felt that if they had the actual choosing of beans or sprouts or whatever, they might show more interest in eating them. Ken, the good model husband, bought the bread and the soft drinks and the couple of bottles of wine and the half-dozen beers. They met at the checkout, loaded up the little car and went bowling. Then they had a burger and chips and went home. They all looked forward to Wednesdays. Judith's friends admired her and said she had the business down to a fine art, their families never thought of shopping as fun. Judith had smiled and secretly congratulated herself. But then it hadn't been very hard, she admitted; because they were so happy almost everything they did was great fun.

She felt slightly dizzy as she sat on the chair near the checkout wondering how she could have got everything so wrong.

The children came up worried to see her sitting down. Normally she was whizzing up and down the aisles at great speed. They checked they had got the right detergent, and the correct cooking foil. Judith forced her face to stay normal, she beat away the wild stare that she knew was threatening to get to the surface. No, she was fine, she said, just a silly cramp, must have bent over the wrong way.

Ken looked at her, pleased.

'Maybe you should sit out the bowling, you don't want to twist yourself and get another stitch.' Had he always spoken like this, a mixture of pity and guilt? Or was it only now? Since Whitsun. Since May the 25th when it all began. Judith gave an involuntary little giggle. The affair would be seven months old on Christmas Day. She wondered would they drink to it. Ken and the woman. The woman she had thought was a friend. She changed the laugh into something more natural.

'I'll be fine,' she said firmly. 'Nothing like a little exercise.' She hoped her smile was natural looking, not like the death's-head grin it felt like from inside.

It was at Whitsun that they went on the holiday to the Leisure Complex. It had sounded such a good idea. Ken had been over-tired at work. There was a lot of pressure in his office. Jane had got very good marks in her term exams at Easter, Tommy had been picked for a tennis team to play for the school. Judith had been promoted to Assistant Manager in the estate agent's: as promotion it didn't mean very much – it was probably an excuse not to give her a big rise – but it looked good on her business card. She had sold a flat to a very nice young woman, Sylvia. Sylvia was a public relations officer for the holiday leisure centre; what could be more natural than that they should make a booking for the long weekend. Sylvia would be there herself, she would keep an eye on Judith and Ken's holiday, she said.

She did that all right.

Judith hadn't realised she would join them for meals so often. But as it turned out she was fun and lively. The children liked her and she was able to get Tommy a game with a really top tennis player and pleaded that Jane be let stay up for the disco.

She linked arms with Judith and took her off to the sauna and swimming pool. She insisted that Ken do several rounds of the nine-hole pitch and putt course even though he had never held a golf club in his life. Then she told him about the driving range. While Ken hit a bucket of golf balls into what he hoped was the far distance but said was only too often the near distance, and Judith had massages and facials, and Jane learned new dances and Tommy played long sustained rallies on the hard courts, Sylvia flitted around them.

Once or twice Judith thought that she must have a lovely life if this swanning around the Leisure Complex was all in the line of duty. But then this was probably just a weekend off, one of the perks of the job that she could come here free whenever she wanted to.

On Whit Monday Sylvia and Ken were gone all day golfing. They came back flushed and happy.

'This has been a highly expensive weekend for me.' Ken had laughed like a boy. 'If I take up golf look at the cost of the gear and the green fees and everything.'

'Look at the saving in executive strain,' Sylvia had argued.

'Why do so many statesmen and executives go out on the golf courses? Look at all you save in terms of tension and Valium.'

Judith had been surprised that Ken had told Sylvia he took tranquillisers to cope with work.

There were so many surprises over the months. None of them important in themselves. All of them part of a picture that Judith had only seen clearly now.

She walked in a semi-daze through the car park to unpack the trolley and stack the boot of the car. Like a mechanical steel arm she received and arranged items, her mind in automatic gear as she placed the bottles standing upwards and wedged them in with softer, sturdier items. It was finished and they walked companionably to the bowling alley as they had done so many Wednesday evenings before. A typical family on an evening out, happier than most, Judith would have said. She would always have said up to fifteen minutes ago.

Sylvia had become part of their life ... how? Through Judith, really. She had been the architect of her own downfall. Yes, she had invited Sylvia to Sunday lunch sometimes, it was lonely for a single woman in London on Sundays. Or if they were having friends to spaghetti on a Friday night she often added Sylvia in. She was so cheerful and lively and somehow everyone else seemed to shine more when she was there. Jane told tales of school instead of staying mute and mutinous and hugging her school world to her like a secret. Tommy confided his hopes to play in the Junior County Championships.

Ken, who hadn't told a funny story about work in years, started doing imitations of the top men at work. It was as if by making fun of them he took the terror out of them, they stopped being demons. Judith herself told marvellous tales about the people who came in to look at houses that were way beyond their price range and how they had to be very tact-ful with a well-known personality who kept insisting on being taken on tours of inspection but who they all knew hadn't a penny in the bank.

Often Judith had felt that Sylvia must envy their family life. She had never married. She did have an affair for a long time with an older man, she confided to Judith, for ten years of her life from the age of twenty-five to thirty-five; she had loved him but then he had tired of her.

'I wouldn't stay around with anyone who didn't want me any longer. I have too much pride,' Sylvia had stated very firmly.

'Of course you didn't have children, that might have made you stay,' Judith had suggested gently.

Sylvia had been adamant. No, even more than ever if she had children. She would not force herself on someone who didn't want her, not at any price. It wouldn't be fair on children either to force them to live in a home without love.

Judith had argued it agreeably, thinking it was one of the many topics they talked about with Sylvia. Like Power and Taste and Class. She was so bright and lifted them out of the humdrum household things they talked about on their own.

But now as she sat shivering in the bowling alley Judith real-ised that Sylvia had not been talking idly. Sylvia had been laying down the lines for the confrontation that was to come. Sylvia was warning Judith not to live in a loveless home.

They had changed their shoes and there was a delay in get-ting a lane. Judith leaned against a wall. It was harder than she thought to keep things sounding normal; she felt sure her face must be flushed and that anyone could see her thoughts.

Only Ken noticed that there was anything amiss.

'You'd tell me if there was anything wrong, if you thought it was anything … well … anything …' he asked.

'Yes, of course I would,' Judith lied at him and looked straight into his eyes. His big kind brown eyes that she had trusted since she met him twenty years ago when they were sixteen. She had trusted him all those years when their parents said they were far too young for each other and when his firm sent him away on a training course. It had never occurred to her that you didn't trust Ken, and here he was with his face full of pain. Pain because he was going to tell her soon. Probably before Christmas. If she could stop him from doing that then things would be all right, or a bit more all right than they were.

It was like not walking on the lines on a pavement. Like when you are on a diet knowing that if you got over the first three days you could stick to it. Somehow if she could stop him telling her then it would mean it wasn't real.

Judith knew that Sylvia would want to be *civilised*. That was one of her great words. Sylvia had little time for those who were not able to take whatever fate or indeed their loved ones handed out in a manner that wasn't *civilised*. Judith had often thought it was a bit harsh to expect someone who had lost everything to go on with life as if nothing had happened. Sylvia had often shrugged and said that surely it was better than tearing each other to bits.

There would be time to think about how *civilised* she would be later, Judith told herself. The most important thing was to have no declaration. No explaining of how for the first time in his life he had found real and true love. No, Ken, not when the whole world was getting ready for Christmas.

Ken touched her hand. 'They're ready for us now, Judith, if you want to?' He had never called her Judy, or Jude; she had loved that, from the start, he had known that when she said her name was Judith, standing there in her school uniform, it was important to her. He liked being called a shortened version of Kenneth, he said it made him seem more like a mate. He had never wanted to feel a person of importance as Judith had. Perhaps that was what had happened, with her petty titles and her making the job in the estate agency sound so powerful. Perhaps he just longed for someone less pompous than her, someone lively and light-hearted like Sylvia.

Perhaps Sylvia was always eager to make love. Judith had been feeling so tired lately. Perhaps Sylvia sounded more interested in his office. Perhaps she encouraged him to do new things, exciting things like taking up golf, when he was only a few short years off forty.

But surely this was nonsense? No agony aunts gave this kind of advice to abandoned wives any more. Did they? Judith felt ashamed that she must have been too smug to read their pages recently. She felt sure that marriages and relationships were based on much more equal terms these days. She didn't feel sure any more of anything.

Automatically she had bowled and somehow the skittles had fallen. Her two children were clapping her eagerly. What kind of life would she give them when their father had left? Would they still come here on a Wednesday? What an empty, pointless evening it would be.

'I honestly don't think you *are* well, Judith, you must sit down quietly.' Ken's voice had never sounded kinder. To her horror she felt her eyes fill with tears.

'I think I must be a bit tired, that's true,' she admitted. 'It's probably work.'

'I used to say that about work too.' He beamed at her. 'But nowadays I just refuse to let it get me down. We are here such a short time.'

There was something ominous in everything he said. Like once upon a time in the days before Sylvia when he had nobody to liven him up, he had been beaten down by work. Like the phrase about life being very short. Judith could hear his speech when he was saying goodbye, it would have a lot about life being short and everyone having to seize what happiness they could find.

At the restaurant she saw him ruffling Tommy's hair and smiling proudly at Jane. He will always love them in that proud, wondering way, Judith thought, even if I am not civilised and fight him over access to them. But she knew she wouldn't fight him over Tommy and Jane. It wouldn't be fair, they were grown people, almost twelve and fourteen. And they'd probably prefer to be with their father and Sylvia anyway.

There was Christmas music in the restaurant too. It seemed like a harsh, cruel mockery to Judith who had always loved Christmas.

She worked like a madwoman in order to keep the house full of people and full of activity. She pretended to be too busy or too tired on the five occasions her husband tried to sit her down alone and tell her that he was going to leave. He even rang her at work.

'I'm going to be in your area, Judith. I wonder could we meet for coffee, or lunch even?'

He was never in her area. He had never taken time for lunch.

'No, Ken,' she had said. 'After Christmas. Please, whatever it is can wait until after Christmas.'

'It can't really,' he said. She felt ice water in her stomach, but she kept the bright tone in her voice.

'It will have to, darling, I'm flat out, on a countdown really. If you'd like me to stay sane let's not try to say anything more complicated than good morning to each other until the festive season is over. All right?' Her voice sounded strange and brittle even to herself.

'That's a very strange way for two people to live together,' Ken had said simply.

She knew he was right. But she could hear the bell-like tones of Sylvia in his voice. She could hear that strong opinionated tone. Little blonde Sylvia, too proud and independent to stay with her older man when he had waned in love. Sylvia for whom everything was absolute.

Judith realised in shock that it was now ten days since they had seen the same Sylvia. In half a year there had never been a gap like this. Under normal circumstances she would have been on the phone after two days to know was everything all right. Judith's pain had dulled a little but it became sharp again thinking of her faithless friend. Sylvia must have agreed to stay out of the picture until Ken had admitted everything, made clear the way and then they could all start being civilised, maybe at Christmas lunch.

It took enormous stamina and great cunning. But apart from when they were alone in the big double bed which they had won in a competition a decade ago when you had to make up a romantic limerick about love, Judith managed to spend no time with her husband.

Some nights when he came to bed she pretended to be asleep and lay long hours listening to his even breathing and the heavy tick of the clock. Two nights she had reached out for him and embraced him so strongly that they were making love before he even realised it. Then afterwards she would have no chat. She said she wanted to lie there in silence. She wondered sometimes what he told Sylvia. Did Sylvia think he was weak, that he was changing his mind?

Judith had no hopes that this was just a fantasy. She had run into Sylvia at the hairdresser. The small attractive face had looked at her quizzically.

'No point in our talking, I suppose?' she had said. 'We'll have to wait until it can all be done in a civilised way.'

Judith hadn't been prepared. If she had, she might have said, 'That will be a very long wait.' As it was she said in a funny breathy tone, 'I know, isn't it dreadful the toll that Christmas takes, we must all be mad really to get so fussed. After Christmas it will all be different.'

'It certainly will,' said Sylvia, her glance never wavering.

Judith had nearly passed out during her hair-do. Her heart was beating so hard she felt that everyone in the salon must be aware of it.

The day arrived. Their house must have been the most beautifully decorated on the street. Their Christmas tree the most splendidly festooned. The cards more artistically arranged than ever, each present wrapped to perfection. The Christmas food was like a spread in a colour supplement showing you how it should be done, each mince pie was scalloped, the bacon rolls to go with the turkey were finished off in identical shape and size as if they were about to go on parade for a royal inspection.

Judith's father and Ken's mother were joining them for lunch. There were candles waiting to be lit, fairy lights on the tree and everything was perfect.

Judith paused with her hands on the back of her chair. This

was probably the last Christmas they would have like this. She would not be able to go to all this trouble if there were no Ken around. The children would grow up and leave eventually. They would have lives of their own, homes of their own. There would be Christmases when they would feel they had to have their mother and make all the arrangements as she and Ken were doing for their father and mother. But her life with Ken was over.

Judith felt a terrible weariness as if the three weeks of frenzied running had caught up with her. She would be too tired now to lift the turkey from the oven, she was too tired to fight. He could tell her whenever he wanted to; the terrible thing was that he was leaving her. After twenty years of knowing him, and sixteen years as his wife she was going to lose this good, kind man. The loneliness was like a terrible ache.

She hadn't noticed him coming in to the room. The others were all in the sitting room, the presents had been opened and were still being admired. He came up and took her hand.

'Please don't run away from me any more. Please. Just for a few short moments. Just for all that we've had together in the past.'

'Very well.' Her voice was just a breath.

'It's not easy.'

'No, Ken, I know it's not.'

'You see, I know you've known. That made it unbearable.'

Somehow it wasn't as bad as she had feared, his saying the words.

She had thought this would be the worst bit, this was what she had been trying to avoid. Now she knew that the worst part was that he was going to leave, that she would be without this kind, good friend and love for ever.

'It's very sad, Ken,' she said. Quite simply, without any disguises, without any accusation. She was just stating a fact.

'I've been so foolish and so cruel and so selfish,' he said. 'I don't know why, maybe it's because I'm no good at anything, not my job, not running a home here, nothing. Maybe that's why I did it.'

'I don't suppose it matters why.' Her voice was heavy now.

'Can you ever forgive me?'

'I suppose we'll all have to be civilised eventually. But it will be a bit hard.' She looked at him pitifully.

His hand came out and he stroked her hair.

'Judith, I'm so sorry.'

'I just didn't want to talk about it before Christmas,' she said.

'And I did, desperately,' he said.

'But I didn't want it to spoil their Christmas for them, I wanted to be able to let them have this one to look back on ...'

'Do they have to know? Why do we have to tell them?' he asked. Humble now.

'But when you've gone ...'

'Do I have to go?' he said.

'You don't want to go?' She looked at him in disbelief.

'Only if you send me away. I'd understand it if you did. We never meant to be unfaithful to each other. You weren't, I was. How are you to believe me when I say it's over and I'm so sorry I could kill myself for hurting you, for being so stupid.'

'You don't love her, you don't want to go?' She said the words in a kind of wonder. The firelight seemed to flicker more brightly on the silver on the table which had been polished until her poor hands had nearly fallen off.

'I don't love her. But can you love me any more when I was

so untrue, so weak and selfish?' His big brown eyes, troubled and guilty, looked at her as she had seen them that day three weeks ago. They were full of shame and guilt but there was hope in them, hope and love.

'I'll be able to love you,' she said. 'Of course I will.'

She put her arms around him and she felt the tiredness leave her. She held him close and stood like that even when the door opened and her son and daughter, her father and her mother-in-law came in.

It didn't matter. It was Christmas. People were allowed to do foolish things when their hearts were full and their hope had not been taken away after all.

Season of Fuss

Mrs Doyle used to begin fussing around October. There was so much to do. The Christmas cakes, the puddings, getting everything out. It drove her children up the wall and down again, particularly since they weren't children any more. They were grown-ups.

It would start when she realised that she had lost Theodora's recipe for the cake, and everything would be turned out on the table. This would reveal new horrors – letters not replied to, knitting patterns that had been promised to friends. All was in disorder, all was confusion, and the very mess that was created served as further proof of how much there was to be done.

'I bought her an album for her recipes,' wailed Brenda. 'I even started cutting them out and putting them in for her, but she actually takes them out again and loses them. It's too bad.'

Brenda's own flat was something that a business efficiency expert would envy. She was always able to retrieve Theodora's recipe for the cake or the last posting dates to America. She would photocopy them for her mother, but it only seemed to add to the fuss. Mrs Doyle would speculate about where she could possibly have put the originals.

Her other daughter, Cathy, used to have to lie down with cold compresses on her eyes after an hour of Mrs Doyle's fussing about the Christmas dinner. To Cathy it was the simplest meal in the whole year. You put a bird into the oven and when it was cooked, you took it out and carved it and ate it. There were potatoes, sprouts, bread sauce, and stuffing to consider, but honestly, unless you were about to throw in the towel, you shouldn't be frightened of that lot. Mrs Doyle would go through her schedule over and over, planning all she should do the night before, and what time she should get up. It was as if she were in charge of mission control at Cape Canaveral instead of lunch for her two daughters and son and two extra spouses. It was a meal for six, not a space shuttle.

Michael Doyle said that he sometimes wanted to lie down on the floor and not get up until Christmas was over when his mother began to talk about the cost of everything. In vain would he urge her not to worry about the price of things. She only had to pay for a turkey and some vegetables. She would have made the pudding and the cake well in advance. Brenda, Cathy, and Michael provided all the wine and the liqueur chocolates, the little extras like a tin of biscuits, or packets of crisps, or a spare set of lights for the Christmas tree to cope with the annual failure of the bulbs to glow.

They all went away drained, back to their houses weary and tense, the spirit of Christmas snuffed out by the buzzing and bustling of the woman who was unable to relax and enjoy the family that gathered around her for Christmas Day.

It was Brenda who decided that this year should be different. Brenda was single and successful at her work and allowed to be a little more bossy than the others. In fact, it was a role she was almost meant to play, and this year she played it for all it was worth.

Cathy had a small baby to think of, a gorgeous five-month-old boy who would be no trouble to anyone, who would sleep peacefully through the hurricane of fuss downstairs, if only Mrs Doyle would allow him to. Cathy was tired this year, unused to the wakeful nights. She should not have to go through all this business with their mother. And Michael's wife, Rose, was pregnant, so she too must not be stressed out by this restless, unsettling atmosphere. She should be allowed tranquillity and a chance to talk about birth and babies to her sister-in-law, Cathy.

In September, Brenda decided on her plan of action. They told Mrs Doyle that as a treat *they* would cook the Christmas meal. Cathy would make the cake, Rose would make the puddings, and on the day Brenda could cook the main course. Mrs Doyle was to put her feet up. They would find a Christmas tree for her and decorate it. They would even buy her Christmas cards well in advance and get the stamps so that she did not have to queue for hours at the post office. Mrs Doyle protested. No, they all said, you've been doing it long enough for us; just this once for a change let us do it instead.

Coming up to Christmas they wondered why this had never occurred to them before. Mrs Doyle was calmer than any of them remembered her having been in her whole life. Sometimes she would begin sentences of urgency, but then she would remember that she had no great onerous duties this year so she would fall silent again. They all lived near enough for her to have a visit from one of them almost every day, and Brenda, Cathy, and Michael congratulated themselves and each other on having reduced the level of fuss by eighty per cent. She still worried about icy roads, and whether she had put enough stamps on the calendar she had sent to her cousin, but that kind of thing was just literally incurable. They had cured all that was available for cure. On Christmas Eve the house looked festive. They had put up a tree, bigger and much better decorated than before. Michael and Brenda had enjoyed doing that, they laughed and poured themselves small vodka-and-oranges. It was like being children again. Cathy had come and decorated the room with holly.

Brian had tacked it up high so that it didn't fall down and scrape people's foreheads, as often happened when Mrs Doyle had tried to shove small spiky bits behind pictures. They had bought cheerful red paper napkins and colourful crackers. Michael had seen to it that there were plenty of briquettes to keep the fire going and an extra box of firelighters. They had set the table for lunch before they left. They kissed Mrs Doyle and looked forward to the happiest Christmas yet.

She walked around the warm, neat house. Brenda had taken the opportunity of doing a little tidying, as well as just getting things ready for the next day's meal. The saucepans that held the potatoes and sprouts were shinier, the turkey with its chestnut stuffing, and sausage-meat stuffing as well, was covered with foil. She was to put it in the oven at eleven a.m. That was all she had to do. Perhaps she might look through that kitchen drawer and sort out some of those old recipes. It would please Brenda to see them in that album. But fancy that! Brenda had already stuck them in for her. The drawers were suspiciously tidy, and though she couldn't actually pinpoint anything that was missing, she felt that a lot of things must have been thrown out.

She would tidy up the food cupboard so that it would impress them when they helped with the washing-up. It was very tidy, actually, and nice clean paper lining the shelves. That was new, surely. Yes, that must have been what Cathy and Rose were doing as they laughed about babies and backache and insisted that Mrs Doyle sit in at the fire out of their way. And her tea towels had all been washed and were stretched over chairs, so that they would be crisp and dry for tomorrow, and a tray had been set for her own breakfast, the boiled egg she would have when she came back from Mass and waited for them to come. Waited doing nothing after she had made the big journey to the oven to put in the turkey at eleven a.m. The day would be so peaceful, compared to other years. They were very good to her, her children. Very good indeed.

She sat down by the fire and thought about James. She even took down his photograph from the mantelpiece and looked at it hard. This was her twelfth Christmas without him. He would only be sixty-two if he were alive, the same age as she was. It wasn't old. A lot of their friends had been older than they were and both husband and wife were still alive. It was far too young to have been twelve years a widow at sixty-two. James shouldn't have died like that. They had hardly had time to say anything to each other and he was gone. Her eyes filled with tears as she heard carol singers going by. Christmas was very hard on widows and people who lived alone.

She was determined not to let her eyes get puffy for tomorrow. Her daughters would peer at her suspiciously and interrogate her.

No. She would remember the good bits of when James was alive; how excited he had been when the children were born; how he had bought drinks for total strangers when his first daughter arrived, and ran around to the neighbours knocking on their windows at the birth of his first son. How he had told everyone of their successes, the number of honours in their exams, the unfairness of Michael's not getting that job because of somebody else's pull. She would think of him coming back from work laughing. She wouldn't think of those last months with the pain and the bewilderment in his eyes, and the constant question, and the constant lying reply. 'Of course you're not going to die, James, don't be ridiculous.'

Somehow this Christmas it was harder to put things out of her mind. She couldn't think why. But it was.

They arrived, arms full of presents, up and down the street people saw that Mrs Doyle was loved and cared for by her children. They saw she had a bright Christmas tree in her window, and they may even have noticed that her brasses were nice and shiny. Brenda had given them a surreptitious rub when her mother wasn't looking.

The lunch was effortless. Their mother sat in her chair, the baby upstairs slept happily through it all, and Michael and Rose talked happily of next Christmas when their own baby would come to the feast. Brenda was the life and soul of the party and said that she had serious designs on a widower who had recently come to the office, and if she played her cards right she might bring him home for Christmas next year.

They all agreed that it had been the happiest Christmas they had spent.

'Since your father died,' Mrs Doyle said.

'Of course,' Michael said hastily.

'Naturally we meant that,' Cathy said.

'Obviously, since Daddy died, that's what we meant,' Brenda said.

They were surprised. Normally she never mentioned Daddy

at Christmas, but she didn't seem upset. It was as if she was saying it for the record.

This time they didn't all rush home. The washing-up was done in relays, with others staying by the big roaring fire talking to Mrs Doyle. There was some television viewing, a walk for everyone except Cathy and Rose, who minded one baby and talked about the next.

There was tea and cake, and much later a small plate of cold turkey with some of Brenda's excellent homemade bread. They all said he would be a lucky widower if Brenda trapped him.

They were gone and the house was warm and tidy still. The wrapping paper had been folded up and stored in the bottom of the dresser. Mrs Doyle could never decide other years whether they should keep it or not; this year the decision had been made for her. Her presents were all on the sideboard. Perfume, talcum, a pen and pencil set, a subscription to a magazine, a hand-embroidered cover for the *RTE Guide*, a bottle of oranges in Grand Marnier, gifts to a woman who was always remembered at Christmas. Why did they make her feel a little uneasy? Perhaps it was the list beside them. Brenda had written out who had given her what. So that there would be no confusion, Brenda had said, when writing to thank. Well, yes. It was useful, of course, but she was sixty-two not ninety-two. They didn't have to put a bib around her neck and feed her. They didn't talk baby language to her. Why write down who gave her what? She had little enough to hold in her mind today. She might have enjoyed thinking over who gave which gift.

Normally Mrs Doyle went to bed exhausted on Christmas night. This year she sat on long at the fireplace and took down the picture of Jim again and wondered why, if God was so good, as the priest had said this morning, he had let Jim suffer for all those months and be so frightened and then let him die. She found no answer to the problem, only guilt at thinking badly of God. She went to bed and lay with her eyes open in the dark for what felt like a long time.

They all dropped in over Christmas week. This had always been the way, they would pop in and out as they felt like it. Usually she would fuss and say she had been about to make scones, but this year it was organised like some military campaign. When Rose and Michael came in the morning, they took her a plate of ham sandwiches just in case anyone dropped in. Then when Cathy and Brian came in the afternoon, hey presto, there was their tea! And Cathy brought a bottle of something that was lemon and cloves and whiskey, you just added hot water. So, lo and behold, when Brenda came by there was a nice unusual little snack for her to try.

But they all thought that something was wrong somewhere. Their mother was too quiet. It wasn't natural for her to be so quiet. She didn't speak until somebody spoke to her. She didn't have any views or complaints or in fact anything at all much to say.

They conferred with each other. It didn't look like flu. She assured them she had no pains and aches. They began to notice it on Stephen's Day and on Thursday it was still there. By Saturday she was positively taciturn.

Brenda worked it out. She had nothing to fuss about, but she also had nothing to do. The central core of their mother's life had become fuss, like the epicentre of a hurricane. Take that away and she was left with nothing. The others wondered was Brenda being too extreme. After all, it had been a wonderful Christmas.

'For us,' Brenda said darkly. 'For us it was.'

On Saturday afternoon she called to see her mother. She had given her no warning and there was nothing prepared. She waited patiently until her mother revved up the fussing batteries and got into the mood where she would sigh and groan and complain about shops being open and not being open and how you never knew which they would be. Brenda nodded in sympathy. She did not produce food from her own well-stocked freezer and larder, as she had been about to do. She allowed the fuss to blow up into a good-sized storm.

Then she played her trump card.

'Are you going to the sales?' she asked. 'They're always so crowded, so hard to decide what to get.'

Mrs Doyle showed a flicker of enthusiasm.

'I don't know why we do it,' Brenda said. 'They're real torture, but on the other hand there are great bargains. Now would you think that it's best to go in first thing on the very first morning with the queues, or do you think that it's better to wait till the rush has died down a bit?'

She was rewarded. Life, a sort of life, had come back to Mrs Doyle's face again. She entered eagerly into the confusion of it all, the exhaustion, the value and the lack of value, the problem of knowing what was rubbish just brought in for the sale and what was a genuine bargain, and as she went to rummage and find the pieces of paper she had cut out during the year about things that would be good value if they were reduced by a third, Brenda sighed and realised that the Season of Fuss had returned and all was well again despite the setback of the perfect Christmas.

'A Typical Irish Christmas ...'

Everyone in the office wanted to ask Ben for Christmas. He was exhausted trying to tell them that honestly he was fine.

He didn't look fine, he didn't sound fine. He was a big sad man who had lost the love of his life last springtime. How could he be fine? Everything reminded him of Ellen. People running to meet others in restaurants, people carrying flowers, people spending a night at home, a night away.

Christmas would be terrible for Ben.

So they all found an excuse to invite him.

For Thanksgiving he had gone to Harry and Jeannie and their children. They would never know how long the hours had seemed, how dry the turkey, how flavourless the pumpkin pie, compared to the way it had been with Ellen.

He had smiled and thanked them and tried to take part, but his heart had been like lead. He had promised Ellen that he would try to be sociable after she was gone, that he would not become a recluse working all the hours of the day and many of the night.

He had not kept his promise.

But Ellen had not known it would be so hard. She would not have known the knives of loss he felt all over him as he sat at a Thanksgiving table with Harry and Jeannie and remembered that last year his Ellen had been alive and well with no shadow of the illness that had taken her away.

Ben really and truly could not go to anyone for Christmas. That had always been their special time, the time they trimmed the tree, for hours and hours, laughing and hugging each other all the while. Ellen would tell him stories about the great trees in the forests of her native Sweden, he told her stories about trees they bought in stores in Brooklyn, late on Christmas Eve when all the likely customers had gone and the trees were half price.

They had no children, but people said this is what made them love each other all the more. There was nobody to share their love but nobody to distract them either. Ellen worked as hard as he did, but she seemed to have time to make cakes and puddings and to soak the smoked fish in a special marinade.

'I want to make sure you never leave me for another woman ...' she had said. 'Who else could give you so many different dishes at Christmas?'

He would never have left her and he could not believe that she had left him that bright spring day.

Christmas with anyone else in New York would be unbearable. But they were all so kind, he couldn't tell them how much he would hate their hospitality. He would have to pretend that he was going elsewhere. But where?

Each morning on his way to work he passed a travel agency that had pictures of Ireland. He didn't know why he picked on that as a place to go. Probably because it was somewhere he had never been with Ellen.

She had always said she wanted the sun, the poor cold Nordic people were starved of sunshine, she needed to go to Mexico or the islands in winter. And that's where they had gone, as Ellen's pale skin turned golden and they walked together, so wrapped up in each other that they never noticed those who travelled on their own.

They must have smiled at them, Ben thought. Ellen was always so generous and warm to people, she would surely have talked to those without company. But he didn't remember it.

'I'm going to Ireland over Christmas,' Ben told people firmly. 'A little work and lot of rest.' He spoke authoritatively, as if he knew exactly what he was going to do.

He could see in their faces that his colleagues and friends were pleased that something had been planned. He marvelled at the easy way they accepted this simplistic explanation. Some months back if a colleague had said he was doing business and having a rest in Ireland, Ben would have nodded too, pleased that it had all worked out so well.

People basically didn't think deeply about other people.

He went into the travel agency to book a holiday.

The girl at the counter was small and dark, she had freckles on her nose, the kind of freckles that Ellen used to get in summer. It was odd to see them in New York on a cold, cold day.

She had her name pinned to her jacket – Fionnula.

'That sure is an unusual name,' Ben said.

He had handed her his business card with a request that she should send him brochures and details of Irish Christmas holidays.

'Oh you'll meet dozens of them when you go to Ireland, if you go,' she said. 'Are you on the run or anything?'

Ben was startled, it wasn't what he had expected.

'Why do you ask that?' he wanted to know.

'Well, it says on your card that you're a vice-president, normally they have people who do their bookings for them. This seems like something secret.'

She had an Irish accent and he felt he was there already, in her country where people asked unusual questions and would be interested in the reply.

'I want to escape, that's right, but not from the law, just from my friends and colleagues – they keep trying to involve me in their holiday plans and I don't want it.'

'And why don't you have any of your own?' Fionnula asked.

'Because my wife died in April.' He said it baldly, as he had never done before.

Fionnula took it in.

'Well, I don't imagine you'd want too much razzmatazz then,' she said.

'No, just a typical Irish Christmas,' he said.

'There's no such thing, any more than there's a typical United States Christmas. If you go to one of the cities I can book you a hotel where there will be a Christmas programme, and maybe visits to the races and dances, and pub tours ... or in the country you could go to somewhere with a lot of sports and hunting and – or even maybe rent a cottage where you'd meet nobody at all, but that might be a bit lonely for you.'

'So what would you suggest?' Ben asked.

'I don't know you, I wouldn't know what you'd like, you'll have to tell me more about yourself.' She was simple and direct.

'If you say that to every client you can't be very cost effective; it would take you three weeks to make a booking.'

Fionnula looked at him with spirit. 'I don't say that to every client, I only say it to you, you've lost your wife, it's different for you, it's important we send you to the right place.'

It was true, Ben thought, he had lost his wife. His eyes filled with tears.

'So you wouldn't want a family scene then?' Fionnula asked, pretending she didn't see that he was about to cry.

'Not unless I could find someone as remote and distant as myself, then they wouldn't want to have anyone to stay.'

'Isn't it very hard on you?' she said, full of sympathy.

'The rest of the world manages. This city must be full of people who lost other people.' Ben was going back into his shell.

'You could stay with my dad,' she said.

'What?'

'You'd be doing me a huge favour if you did go and stay with him, he is much more remote and distant than you are, and he'll be on his own for Christmas.'

'Ah, yes, but . . .'

'And he lives in a big stone farmhouse with two big collie dogs that need to be walked for miles every day along the beach. And there's a grand pub a half a mile down the road, but he won't have a Christmas tree because there'll be no one to look at it but himself.'

'And why aren't you there with him?' Ben spoke equally directly to the girl Fionnula, whom he had never met before.

'Because I followed a man from my home town all the way to New York City, I thought he'd love me and it would be all right.'

Ben did not need to ask if it had been all right, it obviously had been nothing of the sort.

Fionnula spoke. 'My father said hard things and I said hard things, so I'm here and he's there.'

Ben looked at her. 'But you could call him, he could call you.'

'It's not that easy, we'd each be afraid the other would put the phone down. When you don't call that could never happen.'

'So I'm to be the peacemaker.' Ben worked it out.

'You have a lovely kind face and you have nothing else to do,' she said.

The collie dogs were called Sunset and Seaweed. Niall O'Connor apologised and said they were the most stupid names imaginable chosen by his daughter years back, but you have to keep faith with a dog.

'Or a daughter,' Ben the peacemaker had said.

'True, I suppose,' Fionnula's father said.

They shopped in the town and bought the kind of food they would like for Christmas, steak and onions, runny cheese, and up-market ice cream with lumps of chocolate in it.

They went to midnight Mass on Christmas Eve.

Niall O'Connor told Ben his wife had been called Ellen too; they had a good cry together. Next day as they cooked their steaks they never mentioned the tears.

They walked the hills and explored the lakes, and they called on the neighbours and they learned the gossip of the neighbourhood.

There had been no date fixed for Ben's return.

'I have to call Fionnula,' he said.

'She's your travel agent,' Niall O'Connor said.

'And your daughter,' said Ben the peacemaker.

Fionnula said New York was cold but back in business, unlike Ireland which had presumably closed down for two weeks.

'It went great, the typical Irish Christmas,' Ben said. 'I was about to stay on and have a typical Irish New Year as well ... so about the ticket ...?'

'Ben, your ticket is an open ticket, you can travel any day you like ... why are you really calling me?'

'We were hoping that you could come over here and have a quick New Year with us,' he said.

'Who was hoping ...'

'Well, Sunset and Seaweed and Niall and myself to name but four,' he said. 'I'd put them all on to you but the dogs are asleep. Niall's here though.'

He handed the phone to Fionnula's father. And as they spoke to each other he moved out to the door and looked at the Atlantic Ocean from the other side.

The night sky was full of stars.

Somewhere out there two Ellens would be pleased. He took a deep breath that was more deep and free than any he had taken since the springtime.

Travelling Hopefully

They were full of envy at the office when Meg told them she was going to Australia for a month on 11 December.

'The weather,' they said, 'the weather.'

She would miss the cold, wet weeks in London when the streets were so crowded the traffic was at a standstill, when people were fussed and it was also so commercialised.

'Lucky Meg,' they said, and even the younger ones, the girls in their twenties, seemed genuinely jealous of her. This made Meg smile to herself.

Even though she was fifty-three, which didn't feel terribly old, she knew that most of the people she worked with thought she was well over the hill. They knew she had a grown-up son in Australia, but because they knew he was married they weren't interested in him. That, and because he didn't come back home to visit his mum. Married or single they would have been interested had they only seen her handsome Robert. Robert who had been captain of his school, who got so many A levels. Robert, aged twenty-five and married to a girl called Rosa, a Greek girl that Meg had never met.

Robert wrote and said the wedding would be quiet, but it didn't look very quiet, Meg thought, when she got the photographs. There seemed to be dozens and dozens of Greek relatives and friends. Only the groom's family was missing. She tried hard to keep her voice light when she asked him about this on the telephone. He had been impatient, as she had known he would be.

'Don't fuss, Mum,' he had said – as he had said since he was five years old and appeared with blood-soaked bandages around his knee.

'Rosa's people were all here, you and Dad would have had to come thousands of miles. It's not important. You'll come someday when we all have more time to talk.'

And, of course, he had been right. A wedding where most of the cast spoke Greek, where she would have to meet Gerald, her ex-husband, and probably his pert little wife, and make conversation with them ... it would have been intolerable. Robert had been right.

And now she was off to see them, to meet Rosa, the small dark girl in the photographs. She was going to spend a month in the sunshine, see places that she had only seen in magazine articles or on television. They would have a big party to welcome her once she had got over the jet lag. They must think she was very frail, Meg decided; they were giving her four days to recover.

Robert had written excitedly: they would take Meg to the Outback, show her the real Australia. She would not be just a tourist seeing a few sights, she would get to know the place. Secretly she wished he would have said that she could sit all day in the little garden and use the neighbours' swimming pool. Meg had never known a holiday like that. For so many years there had been no holiday at all, as she saved and saved to get

Robert the clothes, the bikes, and the extras that she hoped would make up for the fact that he was missing a father. Gerald had done nothing for the boy except to unsettle him about three times a year with false promises and dreams, and then gave him a battered guitar which had meant more to the boy than anything his mother had worked so hard to provide. It was while playing his guitar during his year in Australia that he had met Rosa and discovered a love and a lifestyle that were going to be for ever, he told his mother.

In Meg's office they clubbed together and bought her a suitcase. It was a lovely light case, far too classy for her, she thought. Not at all the case for someone who never made a foreign journey. She could hardly believe it was hers when she checked it in at the airport. The plane was crowded, they told her, this time of year all the rellies were heading down under.

'Rellies?' Meg was confused.

'People's grannies, you know,' said the young man at the desk.

Meg had wondered whether Rosa might be pregnant. But then they would never be heading for the Outback, wherever it was. She must not ask. She steeled herself over and over not to ask questions that she knew would irritate.

They settled into the plane and a big square man beside her put out his hand to introduce himself.

'Since we're going to be sleeping together in a manner of speaking, I think we should know each other's names,' he said in a broad Irish accent. 'I'm Tom O'Neill from Wicklow.'

'I'm Meg Matthews from London.' She shook his hand, and hoped he wouldn't want to talk for the next twenty-four hours. She wanted to prepare her mind and practise not saying things that would make Robert say 'Don't fuss, Mum.' In fact, Tom O'Neill from Wicklow was an ideal neighbour. He had a small chess set and a book of chess problems. He perched his spectacles on his nose and went methodically through the moves. Meg's magazine and novel remained unopened on her lap. She did a mental checklist. She would *not* ask Robert what he earned a year, whether he had any intention of returning to the academic studies he had abandoned after two years of university, when he went to find himself in Australia and found singing in cafes and Rosa instead. Meg told herself over and over that she would say nothing about how infrequently he telephoned. She wasn't aware that her lips moved as she promised that she would allow no words of loneliness or criticism to escape.

'It's only a bit of air turbulence,' said Tom O'Neill to her reassuringly.

'I beg your pardon?'

'I thought you were saying the Rosary. I wanted to tell you there was no need. Save it till things get really bad.'

He had a nice smile.

'No, I don't say the Rosary actually. How does it work?'

'Irregularly, I would say, like maybe one time out of fifty, but people are so pleased when it does, they think it works all the time and they forget the times it doesn't.'

'And do you say it?' she asked.

'Not nowadays, I did when I was a young fellow. Once it worked spectacularly. I won at the horses, the dogs, and poker. All in one week.' He looked very happy at the memory.

'I don't think you were meant to pray about those kinds of things. I didn't think it worked for gambling.'

'It didn't in the long run,' he said ruefully, and went back to his chess.

Meg noticed that Tom O'Neill drank nothing and ate little; he had glass after glass of water. Eventually she commented on it. The meals were one of the few pleasures of long-haul flying, and the drink would help sleep.

'I have to be in good shape when we arrive,' he said. 'I've read that the secret is buckets and buckets of water.'

'You're very extreme the way you take things,' Meg said to him, half admiring, half critical.

'I know,' Tom O'Neill said, 'that has been the curse and the blessing of my life.'

There were still fifteen hours to go. Meg didn't encourage any stories of his life. Not so early in the trip. When they had only four hours left she began to ask him about his life. It was a story of a daughter who had been wild. Once the girl's mother had died, Tom hadn't been able to control her. The girl had done what she liked when she liked. Now she was living in Australia. Not just staying there, mind, but living there. With a man. Not a husband, but what they called a De Facto. Very liberal, very modern, his daughter living with a man openly and telling the Australian government this too, proud as punch. He shook his head, angry and upset by it all.

'I suppose you will have to accept it. I mean coming all this way, it would be a bit pointless if you were to attack her about it,' Meg said. It was so easy to be wise about other people's business.

She told him in turn about Robert, and how she hadn't been invited to the wedding. Tom O'Neill said wasn't it a blessing? She'd have had to make conversation with her ex and a lot of people who hadn't a word of any language between them. Much better to go now. What was a wedding day? It was only a day – not that he seemed likely to be having the opportunity of seeing one in his circumstances.

His daughter was called Deirdre, a good Irish name, but now she signed herself Dee, and her man friend was called Fox.

What kind of name was that for a human being?

The blinds were raised. They had orange juice and hot towels to wake them up. Meg and Tom felt like old friends by this stage. They were almost loath to part. As they waited for their luggage they gave each other advice.

'Try not to mention their wedding day,' Tom warned.

'Don't say anything about the living-in-sin bit. They don't think that way here,' she begged.

'I wrote out my address,' he said.

'Thank you, thank you.' Meg felt guilty that she hadn't thought to write her son's address. Perhaps it was because she did not want Robert to think she was pathetic, picking up a strange Irishman on the plane and giving him her phone number.

'I'll leave it to you then ... to get in touch or whatever,' he said, and she could sense the disappointment in his voice.

'Yes, yes, what a good idea,' Meg said.

'It's just a month is a long time,' he said.

Earlier they had both told each other that it was a very short time. Now they were on Australian soil and both of them slightly nervous of meeting their children ... it seemed too long.

'It's in Randwick,' Meg began.

'No, no, you ring me if you'd like a cup of coffee someday. Maybe we could have a bit of a walk and a chat.'

He looked frightened. The endless glasses of water had left him in no state to deal with a man called Fox on equal terms. He didn't look like a man who was going to remember that his daughter called herself Dee and that she thought she *was* married, a De Facto being more or less the same. Meg felt protective of him.

'Certainly I'll call you. In fact, I think we will both possibly need to escape a little from the culture shock,' she said.

She knew she looked anxious. She could feel the frown

developing on her forehead, the squeezing of her eyebrows together which made people at work say that Meg was getting into a tizz, and made her son beg her to stop fussing. She wished she could go on talking to this easy man. Why couldn't they sit down on chairs and talk for an hour or so, get themselves ready for a very different kind of Christmas than they had ever had before, and for a different lifestyle.

She realised suddenly that this was what they were both doing. They were coming to give their blessing to new lifestyles. Tom was here to tell Dee that he was glad she had found Fox and he didn't mind about their not being married properly. She was here to tell Robert that she couldn't wait to meet her new daughter-in-law and all her family, and not to hint that she ever gave her absence from their actual wedding day a thought. It would be good to meet Tom again and to know how it was all going. If they had been old friends, then obviously they would have done, but being single and middle-aged and having just met on the plane it would call for many more explanations. Possibly Robert would pity her. Or else Rosa would think that it was wonderful, perhaps, that Mother had actually found herself a bloke on a plane trip. In either case it would have been embarrassing.

'I thought I might tell Deirdre, *Dee*, her name is Dee. Lord God, I must remember her name is Dee,' Tom began.

'Yes?'

'I thought I might tell her that you and I were friends from way back. You know?'

'I know,' she said, with a very warm smile.

They could have said more, a great deal more. In fact, they needed to find out a bit more about each other if they were meant to be friends. But it was too late. They were wheeling their trolleys through the passage to where a crowd of suntanned, healthy-looking young Australians waited for the crumpled rellies to stagger from the long journey. And people were calling and crying out and raising children up in the air to wave. And it seemed to be the middle of summer.

And there was Robert in shorts with long, suntanned legs and his arm around the neck of a tiny little girl with huge eyes and black curly hair biting her lip anxiously as they raked the crowd to find Meg; and when they saw her, Robert shouted, 'There she is!' as if nobody else had travelled all those hours on the plane, and they were hugging her and Rosa was crying.

'You are so young, too young to be a grandmother,' she said, and patted her little tummy with such pride that Meg started to cry too. And Robert held her and didn't ask her not to fuss. Over her son's shoulder Meg could see Tom O'Neill's beautiful daughter, the girl who had been wild all her life but didn't look wild any more. Dee was shyly introducing a round-faced, red-headed, bespectacled boy who was loosening the unaccustomed collar and tie he had put on specially to meet the father-in-law from Ireland. Tom was indicating the boy's hair, making some joke maybe about how he knew now why he was called Fox. Whatever he said, they were all laughing.

And now Robert and Rosa were laughing too as they wiped their tears and led her towards the car. Meg looked back in case she could catch the eye of her friend Tom O'Neill, the old friend she had met by chance on the plane. But he, too, was being bundled off. It didn't matter. They would meet here in Australia, maybe two or three times so that they would not always be in the young people's way. But not too often, because a month was a very short time for a visit. And Christmas was for families. And anyway they could always meet back on the other side of the world in a time and a place where there wouldn't be so much to do.

What Is Happiness?

They had called him Parnell to show how Irish he was. At school they called him Parny, so that was it. Anyway Katy and Shane Quinn could always explain it to anyone who mattered that his real name was Parnell, like the great leader. It was just as well nobody asked them too much about the great leader. They were somewhat hazy about what he was leading and when and why. They liked the Parnell Monument when they came to Dublin, but they didn't like at all the news that the great leader had been a Protestant, and a womaniser. They hoped that this was just a local story.

Parny liked Dublin, it was small and kind of folksy. People seemed poor compared to at home and it was hard to find the downtown area, but it was much better than being at home for Christmas. Much much better.

At home there would have been Dad's receptionist, Esther. Esther had worked for Dad for nine years, since Parny was a baby. Esther was a wonderful receptionist but a sad, lonely person according to Dad. Esther was a nutter who was in love with Parny's father according to Mom. Last Christmas, Esther had come to the house and sat down on the doorstep and cried until they had to let her in for fear of the neighbours complaining. She had shouted at them and gone round and banged on windows. Esther had said that she would not be cast aside. They had all asked Parny to go to bed.

'But I've only just got up. It's Christmas Day, for the Lord's sake!' he had cried, not unreasonably. They begged him to go back to bed with his toys. He agreed grudgingly because his mom had whispered that mad Esther would go sooner. He had listened on the stairs, of course, it had been very bewildering indeed.

He gathered that Dad must have had a romance with Esther at one stage. It sounded impossible what with Dad being so old, desperately old now, and with Esther looking like she did, terrible. And it seemed hard to know why Mom was so upset, she must be well finished with Dad now. But that was definitely what it was about.

There were enough kids at school who had moms and dads split up for him to know about this, and Esther kept shouting that Dad had promised to divorce Mom as soon as the brat was old enough. Parny was very annoyed to be called a brat and bristled on the stairs, but both Mom and Dad seemed very annoyed too and had rushed to his defence, so Esther had lost out on that one, and at least his parents seemed to be on his side. Parny gave it up after a while and had gone back to his room to play with his presents as they had advised.

'I want some happiness. I want to be happy too,' he heard Esther shouting downstairs. 'What's happiness, Esther?' he had heard his father asking wearily.

They had been right, it was the best thing for him to go upstairs. Later when she was gone, they came to get him. They were full of apologies. Parny was more interested in it all than frightened.

'Did you plan to divorce Mom and go off with her, Dad?' he enquired, for the record, as it were. There was a lot of bluster.

Eventually Dad said, 'No, I told her I would, but I didn't mean it. I told her a lie, son, and I'm paying for it dearly.'

Parny nodded. 'I thought that was it,' he said sagely. Mom was pleased with this explanation of Dad's. She patted Dad's hand.

'Your father is a mighty brave man to admit that, Parny,' she said. 'Not all men are so severely punished for straying from the home.'

Parny said that having Esther screaming on the doorstep was a terrible punishment all right. Did she scream and rave in the surgery too? he wondered.

No, apparently not, she was nice and calm and official when wearing her white coat. It was only in leisure times and particularly high holidays that she became upset and carried on. Labor Day and Thanksgiving she had called, but she had not been so disturbed. During the year Esther had come to the house again; she came on New Year's Eve, and on Dad's birthday and in the middle of the St Patrick's Day party they held, and they saw her turning up for the Fourth of July picnic just as they were unpacking the barbecue, and Dad and Mom had leapt back into the car and they had driven for miles looking over their shoulder in case she was behind.

So this year, to escape her, they had come to Ireland. They had always wanted to visit the home of their ancestors, they had said, but now with Parny being old enough to appreciate everything, well, why not? And actually things were getting very urgent now. At this year's Thanksgiving Esther had arrived wearing a spaceman suit and they thought she was a singing telegram and opened the door. Then she was in like a flash.

So that's why they were in the land of his ancestors at last. Parny was glad, he missed his friends at Christmas but he was becoming as edgy as Mom and Dad about any celebration in case he saw the red mad face of Esther appearing.

He had half hoped she would turn up at his own birthday. It would have been something for the school to talk about for months. But she didn't. It was only official celebrations and Dad's birthday. She must be nearly mad enough to be put away, Parny thought. Seriously he wondered why nobody had. 'She had nobody to put her away,' Mom had explained.

Parny thought this might be Esther's bit of good luck. If you had had as much bad luck as she had, then maybe it was only fair that fate should deal you the good card of having nobody around to get you locked up. She could roam free for a bit longer.

He asked why Dad couldn't fire her. Dad said there were laws about this sort of thing, and if Esther was a very good worker, which she was, and not at all mad in the office, if he fired Esther there would be a huge protest and he might be sued.

Dad and Mom seemed nice and relaxed now that there was no Esther. Parny saw that they held hands sometimes, which was very embarrassing to watch, but at least there was nobody here that would know them so it was okay.

The hall porter became a great friend of Parny's: he told the boy all about the days when there were dozens and dozens of American tourists staying in the hotel, when they came and hired his brother out to drive them all over Ireland and then back to the hotel again. The porter's name was Mick Quinn, and he said it was an undeniable fact that he and Parny must be some kind of relations, otherwise why would they be called the same name? Mick Quinn had all the time in the world to spare for Parny since the hotel was almost empty, and Parny's Mom and Dad were given to looking into each other's eyes and having long conversations about life.

This was all to the good. Parny used to go with Mick to collect the newspapers in the morning and helped with the luggage; he even got a tip once.

He was most useful to Mick by holding the cigarettes. Mick wasn't supposed to smoke on duty, so it just looked as if Parny was a forward American brat allowed to do what he liked, including smoking at the age of ten.

Parny was great at sidling up when the coast was clear to give Mick a drag. Mick was married to a woman called Berna. Parny asked a lot about Berna. 'She's not the worst,' Mick would say. 'Who *is* the worst?' Parny always wanted to know. If Berna wasn't, someone must be the worst, but Mick said it was only a manner of speaking. Mick and Berna had grown-up children now, they were away, all of them. Three in England, one in Australia, and one at the other side of Dublin – which was the same as being in Australia.

What did Berna do all day when Mick was in the hotel? Parny wondered. His mom worked in a flower shop, which was very smart and a perfectly fine place for a dentist's wife to work. But Berna worked nowhere.

She spent the day in a state of discontent, Mick revealed one time. She didn't know the meaning of happiness. But he seemed ashamed he had told Parny this and never wanted to bring the subject up again.

'What is happiness exactly, Mick?' Parny asked.

'Well, if you don't know, a fine young fellow like you who

has everything he wants, then it would be hard for the rest of us to know.'

'I suppose I do have a lot of things,' Parny said. 'But then so has Esther, and not only is she not happy but she's crazy as a box of birds.'

'I don't think there is anything crazy about a box of birds,' Mick said unexpectedly.

'No, neither do I,' said Parny. 'It's like you said about Berna not being the worst. It's only a manner of speaking.'

'I'm very fond of birds in fact,' Mick Quinn said, having a quick drag out of Parny Quinn's cigarette. 'I'd have liked pigeons, but Berna said they were dirty.' He shook his head sadly and Parny felt that Berna must be very nearly the worst.

'Who is this Esther anyway?' Mick said, anxious to drag his thoughts and conversation away from the unsatisfactory Berna.

'It's all too long and complicated to explain, unless we had time,' Parny said. You couldn't do justice to the madness of Esther in the fairly uneasy atmosphere of the hall, waiting for a manager to appear suddenly or a guest to need some assistance and advice.

In fact something made Parny wonder if his new friend Mick would ever understand about Esther. 'Maybe you might like to come on a tour with me this afternoon, you could tell me then?' Mick said.

'Yes, and you could tell me about the birds you might have,' Parny said.

'I'll show you some birds, that would be better still.'

Parny's mom said they had been neglecting him. She and Dad had been feeling very guilty, but they had many important things to talk about. This very afternoon they would take him to a movie house. He could choose which one and if they could bear his first choice, they would all go to that, but if they really couldn't bear his first choice, they might ask him to make a second choice. Parny said that he and Mick were going to visit some birds.

'That means girls in this part of the world,' Parny's dad said.

'No.' Parny was very clear on this, it didn't. Not with Mick. Mick had his fill of women, he had Berna who was always in a state of discontent, he wanted no more truck with women, he had told Parny that personally.

Parny's mom thought Mick had made a right choice. She looked meaningfully at Parny's dad and said sooner or later most men come to that conclusion.

Mick looked different in his ordinary clothes, not as splendid as in the porter's uniform, but he said he felt free as a seagull that soared when he put on his old jacket and trousers. He led Parny to a bus. 'Is it an aviary?' Parny asked, interested.

'No. It's more a house of a fellow. I have a part interest in some pigeons. Hardly anyone knows that except you and me,' Mick said, looking round in case anyone on the bus might have heard it and confronted them with the information. 'They don't know at the hotel,' he whispered.

'Would they mind?' Parny whispered back. He didn't see the harm in having a part interest in pigeons. But it was obviously fraught with danger.

'I just don't want them to know my business. They'd be asking how are the pigeons. I couldn't be doing with that.'

Parny understood immediately. To have people who knew nothing about it asking, would diminish the pigeons. 'I'm afraid I'm not what you'd call an expert myself,' he said, in order to make sure there were no grey areas.

'I know that, son, but you have an open mind. A young open mind.'

'Esther said that to me once. She said I had a young mind that wasn't closed up like the older generation.' He was lost in wonderment that here at the other side of the earth someone should say exactly the same thing to him. He hoped this didn't mean that Mick was crazy, too, like Esther. 'Have you anyone to put you away if you go mad?' he asked solicitously.

Mick was delighted with him. 'You're a living entertainment, Parny Quinn. Who's Esther, is she your sister?' Parny noticed that they asked each other questions and never replied one to the other. It didn't matter somehow, the questions weren't that important. They got off the bus and went into a house that seemed rather poor to Parny. He hoped it wasn't Mick's house, he'd like Mick to have had more comfort. 'Is this where you live?'

'Indeed not.' Mick sounded wistful, looking at the shabby cupboards and the piles of newspapers on the floor, the dishes on the draining board, and the empty milk bottle on the table. 'No, I live at a place where you have to take off your shoes almost. No indeed, in my house there'd be a commotion that you'd hear at the other end of the country if I brought you in without an act of Parliament being passed first. This is Ger's house.' He said it with pure envy.

Ger was out in the back. He seemed pleased to see Parny, asked him was he a betting man, and Parny said he was sure he would be when he was old enough to know what to bet on and to have some money to bet with. Ger accepted this as a reasonable answer and didn't apologise for having assumed that Parny was rarely out of a bookie's office. Ger was an all-right guy, Parny thought to himself.

They showed him the loft, they explained the rules. Man to

man, the three of them discussed the singularly poor record of Ger and Mick's pigeons compared to other pigeons they knew and envied. They were homing pigeons certainly, the backyard was full of them, but would they go back into the box? Would they hell! Race after race could have been won if these birds could only have followed the rules. But no. Instead they came and sat and cooed in the yard, delighted to be back to Ger and Mick. Some of them were definitely not the full shilling, Parny was told though it was a view that would not be expressed beyond these four walls. Parny had to admit that he didn't know whether there was any pigeon fancying in the States, but he would enquire when he got back, he would write and tell Ger and Mick all about it.

'A young fellow like you won't think of writing,' Ger said philosophically as the pigeons swooped down on Parny and perched on his shoulders, glad to have a new playmate in this friendly place, a playmate that didn't seem obsessed with their timings.

'I'm very good at writing letters,' Parny protested. 'I've written to everyone I said I would ...' He paused. 'Well, except Esther.'

'I think you'd better tell us about Esther,' Mick Quinn said.

In the small backyard with the big soft birds landing and taking off, with the comforting warbling sound of their cooing as Muzak in the background, Parny Quinn told Ger and Mick about Esther. He could never have asked for a better audience, it was like telling a film, they said to each other as they demanded details of her appearance at each festivity. Would you credit that? The family had to cross the Atlantic to escape her.

'And why would she want you to write to her?' Mick asked eventually.

'The day before we left, she said she knew we were going somewhere, and would I write her just one letter, to let her know if we had found happiness wherever it was we had gone. But I couldn't write. I couldn't tell Esther that Mom and Dad look sort of happy with all this awful holding hands. She'd flip completely if she knew that.'

He stood there as the pigeons came and went, he stroked their feathers and they didn't seem frightened, he held one in his hand and felt its heart beat under its plump chest. He closed his eyes as they swirled around. There wasn't much to beat this, the company of birds and men. Undemanding, satisfying. He had a feeling that he might never be as happy as this again.

'You could send the poor woman a card,' Mick said.

'Not committing yourself to anything,' said Ger, who had always travelled alone in life and thought it was the best way to be.

'It's too late now. We're going back on Friday, it won't get there.'

'We could ring her from the hotel,' Mick said.

'Call Esther? Mom would turn blue and die,' Parny said.

'Without telling your ma.'

'I wouldn't be able to afford it, calling the States is very expensive.' Ger and Mick nodded at each other. It could be done, they said. If he had anything to say to the poor tortured woman, then at Christmastime, the season of goodwill, he should say it.

Parny wondered had he explained how crazy Esther was, and how she wanted to run away with his father. But still Mick and Ger were so kind, it would be very bad-mannered to go against them.

The afternoon passed in a welter of feathers and timings and soft sounds. Then it was back on the bus to the hotel. It was six o'clock, so it would be Esther's lunchtime. From the phone box in the hall Parny talked to the international operator, they found directory enquiries and they found Esther. Parny also enquired how much it would cost and had to hold on to the door of the box for support. He told Mick it was out of the question. Mick was back in his uniform again, he worked a split shift some days, he had only the afternoon free. He looked up and down the hall.

'Get back in the box,' he said, and like lightning he dialled from the desk the number written on a piece of paper. Parny heard the phone ringing, he swallowed. Esther's voice was surprisingly thin, not like the excited roar he had come to know and fear.

'It's Parny Quinn,' he said.

Esther began to cry, softly, it was definitely crying.

'Did your father ask you to call me?' she sniffled.

'He doesn't know I'm calling you. Listen, Esther, the mail is very bad here, and you asked me to let you know about happiness and everything ...'

'What's happiness?' Esther said.

Parny was impatient. Why do people always say that, he was calling her long distance to answer her damn fool questions, now she just asks them back.

'Yeah sure, it's hard to know, but you did ask me to let you know if I'd found it, so I thought I'd call you and say it has a lot to do with birds.'

'Birds?'

'Yes, birds, pigeons, you could go to the library and get a book on them. I think you'd enjoy that, honestly, Esther.'

'Has your father taken up the bird business too?'

'No, Esther, just me, you wanted to know what I thought and if I had found happiness. I did, so I thought I'd call you.'

He was annoyed that she was ungrateful. 'Who cares what you think, kid?' Esther said. 'Put me on to your father.'

'He's not here,' Parny said, tears of rage stinging the back of his eyes. After all his kindness and Mick risking his job connecting him on the hotel phone. 'Dad and Mom are in Dublin Casino, they're not back yet.'

'You're in Dublin,' Esther screamed triumphantly. 'What hotel, speak to me, Parnell, you dumb child. Speak. What hotel?'

Parny hung up. Mick was waiting outside. 'You did your best, lad, you kept faith with her. And there's always the pigeons as consolation, remember that.'

Esther got a list of hotels in Dublin and she had found Katy and Shane Quinn by seven p.m.

'I guess she must have traced us through the airlines or travel agent,' Parny's pop said.

'They really will have to put her away this time,' said Parny's mom with a grim little smile.

'Fancy saying that Parny called her.'

'She seemed very definite about that.' Parny's dad sighed. 'Said he'd called her up to tell her that he had taken up ornithology. It's sad, really sad.'

'I wonder why she fixed on Parny this time. She's always steered clear of talking about you, she knows how upset it makes us.'

Parny sat there thinking about the events of the day. It could have been worse. Esther couldn't get a flight what with it being Christmas, she was just going to haunt them by telephone. Dad had to ask the switchboard to say we had left the hotel. Parny had said nothing about his part in it all. He had thought it through very carefully. If they thought she was making it all up about his having called her, that would be further proof of her madness. It might speed up the day they put her away. And anyway he hadn't been going to say anything about Ger and Mick's part share in the pigeons. He remembered that Mick never spoke of the pigeons in the hotel, they were too precious. Parny felt like that too.

Anyway Esther had called him a dumb kid and said nobody cared what he thought about anything. Why should he bail her out? Why should he? He would keep his interest in pigeons a secret, just like Mick did, and one day when Esther was safely locked up he would pretend to have read a book about them, and he'd have his own loft. And he would have no truck with women. Ever. You could see that Ger in his free-and-easy house was like a king compared to people like his father and Mick who were heart-scalded.

Parny sighed happily and read the movie listings. He liked the sound of *The Company of Wolves*, but you had to be eighteen to get in. He wondered could he tell the people at the cinema that he was from the States and more mature than other kids of his age.

The Best Inn
in Town

They should have liked each other, the two mothers. They were birds of the same showy kind of feather, after all. Full of notions, full of what they each liked to think of as style. But they hated each other the very moment they met eighteen long years ago when their respective son and daughter got engaged to each other. Noel's mother, who became Granny Dunne a year later, had a lip that curled all on its own without being given any instructions; and Avril's mother, who had become Granny Byrne, had a line in tinkling laughs that would freeze the blood. They had both had husbands back at the wedding, mild men who managed to put the children's happiness before their own territorial struggles, but not even the shared experience of widowhood had brought the two women together. They met one day a year, and that was Christmas Day. They met to terrorise and destroy what might have been a fairly reasonable family Christmas.

Noel was called Noel because he was a Christmas baby. Granny Dunne never tired of telling that. How the pains had come during Christmas lunch. How there had been mistletoe and holly and paper streamers all around the maternity ward. Oh, they knew how to celebrate Christmas in those days, she would say accusingly to Avril, as if a labour ward in those days was somehow like the Versailles Ball in comparison with the kind of entertainment she was being offered these times.

Granny Byrne never failed to explain that Avril had been given her name because she was born in April. A lovely month, full of sunshine and fresh flowers, and little lambs and everything full of hope. In those days. There would be a sad, chilling tinkle of a laugh and a glower at Noel. The implication was easy to read. Life had lost its spring freshness since her daughter had married at the age of nineteen and thrown away all that hope for ever.

Noel and Avril had triumphed over their mothers' great mutual dislike. In fact it had cemented them further together over the years. They were lucky, they said, in that the scales were fairly evenly balanced. For every one of Granny Dunne's clangers there was a reciprocal salvo from Granny Byrne. And they were careful to treat each mother equally so that no comparisons could be made. On the first Sunday of each month they visited one or the other parent alternately. The three children liked Granny Dunne's house because she had an aquarium, and Granny Byrne's house because she had a Manx cat and a book about Manx cats which they would read six times a year with total fascination.

No, it was no trouble for the children going to either granny's house. For Noel and Avril it was always a trial. Granny Dunne had a very strong line about cats spreading diseases and that if you had to have a cat, wasn't it perverse getting a poor dumb animal that was bred deformed and had its nether regions on display. Granny Byrne always managed to bring up what she thought of people who had warm tanks of stale water and poor crazed orange fish in them swimming despairingly around for the sole purpose of being soothing for neurotic humans.

Granny Byrne usually said it was wonderful that Avril managed so well without all the newest modern appliances which most husbands bought for their wives. Avril just gritted her teeth and squeezed Noel's hand to show him that her mother was not mouthing her own discontents. Then Granny Dunne would say, with a lip curl that might have remained permanent if the wind changed, that she really admired young women like her daughter-in-law who didn't bother with make-up and dressing properly just to please their man and do him credit. Noel's turn for hand-squeezing would come then. They agreed that they were forced into a great deal of reassurance and positive stating that they loved each other, just to counteract the effects of both mothers. And that this might be no bad thing.

They had called their children Ann, Mary, and John as a reaction against their own fancy tricksy names. Both mothers thought these names sadly unimaginative and each blamed the child of the other for the lack of vision and style.

Ann was seventeen and had been put in charge of the entertainment programme for Christmas Day. Ann was good at computer studies at school, which was a help because it was becoming more and more difficult to organise the grannies' entertainment. The problem was the increase in television channels and the availability of videos. This Christmas there was far too much choice. Ann explained seriously to her parents that it had been much simpler in the days when it was only *The Sound of Music* and then the usual row about the Pope and the Queen. Avril's mother, Granny Byrne, thought that anyone with a bit of class watched the Queen's Message; it was nothing to do with being pro-English or West Brit or anything, it was just what one did. Noel's mother said it had never been part of their culture to watch the Royal Family. But then she did remember that a long time ago the maids in the house had indeed been very interested in reading little titbits about royalty, so perhaps some people did find it all very fascinating. For her own part, even though she didn't go along with every single thing about the Pope, she did think it would be a poor sort of Catholic who couldn't find it in her heart to kneel for a papal blessing just one day out of three hundred and sixty-five.

Noel and Avril had stayed sane by incorporating both dignitaries into their Christmas Day. There were other ingredients too, like a good healthy walk after the Pope and before the mince pies and presents. They had agreed it would be straitjackets for supper if they had to remain cooped up all day. Even in the rain or the snow they got the show on the road and down to the strand. They used to walk past other families, and Noel and Avril often wondered if they were really happy or whether each family group was like their own, a powder keg, a volcano, a collection of disasters waiting to happen.

And then, after the heavy cocktails which went with the Queen there was the Christmas lunch, and Serious Viewing combined with snoozing, until the Good-Lord-is-that-the-time? What about a nice cup of tea and Christmas cake before we drive you both home?

Since they had got the video, life had been easier. It wasn't a question of zapping from channel to channel, nor of trying to decide on the spot. For the past couple of years the family had studied the advance Christmas schedules with the intensity that had been given to the Normandy landings. Pop shows were out because of the torrent of abuse they would unleash. Comedy shows were doubtful. They wouldn't be worth all the side looks and wondering if Granny Byrne had got the point or if Granny Dunne was about to say that for the life of her she couldn't understand people who took offence over nothing. It was always impossible to programme the grannies. One year one would have a high moral tone and the other have become bawdy, but you never knew which would be which. It was like the Christmas presents, a feast or a famine. Indulge them while they're young, or give them a sense of proportion.

Ann felt very important to be allowed to choose the entertainment, but she admitted that there were a lot of problems. If they recorded *Back to the Future* on one channel during lunch, then it would be ready to watch at five o'clock, but could the grannies take a time machine on board?

The children would like to see *The Empire Strikes Back*, Ann reported. They had been hoping that she would be able to fit it into the recording plan. But it went on from four till six and probably they'd need to be watching something then, and most likely something already on a video, so that meant they wouldn't be able to record at the same time.

Ann wondered if they might record *Storm Boy* earlier; it sounded more suitable family viewing than *Falling in Love*. They didn't know what *Falling in Love* was going to be about, but if it had Meryl Streep and Robert De Niro there could be a lot of groping involved, and nobody knew how the grannies might respond to screen fondling.

Noel and Avril watched their daughter's serious face as she juggled the schedules. The music programmes that Mary and John loved had to be out; the grannies couldn't take anything like that. There was a game show that was described as a Christmas frolic, and it was always unwise to think that a frolic might please either Mrs Dunne or Mrs Byrne. There were the soaps, obviously, but not the Christmas variety show – it was too varied. They might love the choirboys singing carols but would it be worth it for the tirades that might erupt at the more modern acts?

Ann said she'd consult again with the younger ones: there had to be a way. All families must have the same problems at this time of year, she said sagely, it was just that the youngsters kept bleating about *Top of the Pops* and other things that were out of the question. It wasn't as if Christmas was meant to be for children.

Avril and Noel's hearts were filled with sadness. Their daughter was not being even remotely ironic. All her life she had thought that Christmas Day had to do with the grannies and keeping them as contented as either would allow herself to be.

Avril bit her lip at the memory at what seemed like a thousand Christmas days when Granny Dunne had looked her up and down and asked her when she was going to change, and then with a lip curl apologised and said of course, of course, she had changed, and how sensible she was not to get dressed up in anything smart.

She remembered another thousand festive seasons when Granny Byrne had examined the label on the supermarket wine bottle and asked Noel who his wine merchant was and had they chosen something special this year. A thousand times Noel had patted her hand under the table. It didn't matter, he had told her. We have all our lives.

True, but their children were not having the Christmas Days they should have been having.

If there were no grannies, think what it would be like. Think.

Avril indulged herself. They could get up later, they could

have breakfast in their dressing gowns. Cup after cup of tea watching the video of *Fawlty Towers*. The episode of Manuel's rat. They all loved that. There would be no sneaking glances at the two good armchairs to see how it was being received.

They could all have a short walk and wear old clothes and maybe go somewhere with a bit of mud and point things out to each other and laugh. Like they did on ordinary days. Not walking at Granny speed and fielding a battery of Granny interrogation and point-scoring.

They need watch neither Pope nor Queen. Their Christmas messages would be in their own family.

The turkey would taste better when it didn't have to be analysed and explained and apologised for. They could have Greek yogurt with the Christmas pudding, which they all loved instead of making a brandy butter for show. The children could laugh out loud at the jokes in the crackers instead of nodding sagely with the grannies that it was a sin crying out to heaven for vengeance buying crackers that were such poor value.

Noel too felt a surge of resentment toward his two brothers and his sister who never thought of having Mother for Christmas. Not even once. It's tradition that she goes to Noel and Avril, they all said with huge guilty relief, and gave her bottles of sherry and fleece-lined hot-water bottles plus tiny boxes of liqueur chocolates, which she was instructed to keep for herself and which she did.

And couldn't Avril's sister in Limerick take Mrs Byrne? Just once, just one year? Why did it have to be a tradition? The old bats would even *like* a change, a bit of variety, Noel thought despairingly.

But it was too late this year to think about it. The plans would have to be made long in advance, and it must never be allowed to look like ... well, to look like what it was.

Avril and Noel looked at each other and for once they didn't reach out to pat, to reassure, to remind each other of a lifetime shared and to underline that one day wasn't much to give up. For the first time, it did seem too much. The day that everyone was meant to enjoy; and their family seriously believed that it wasn't meant to be a day for children.

The feeling lasted through the days that led up to Christmas. The children knew there was something wrong. Their mother and father, normally so full of requests and pleas and urgings, seemed to have lost the Christmas spirit somehow.

They didn't even have those embarrassing middle-aged hugs and hand-pattings that used to go on. When Ann or Mary or John asked about plans for the grannies, they got scant answers.

'Will we bring down the screen in case Granny Byrne gets a draught?' Ann asked.

'Let her get a draught,' her mother said unexpectedly.

'Where's the magnifying glass for the *RTE Guide*?' John asked on Christmas Eve. 'Granny Dunne likes to have it handy to see the small print.'

'Then let her put on her bloody glasses like the rest of us,' said his father.

They were very worried about them.

Ann thought her father might be having the male menopause: Mary wondered whether their mother might be having a mid-life crisis. She didn't know what it was, but there had been a programme about it on television with lots of white-faced women of their mother's age saying they were going through it. John thought they were just in bad tempers like teachers at school got into bad tempers that seemed to last half a term. He hoped his parents would get over it. It was very glum with them like this, biting the head off everyone.

The night before Christmas the family sat beside the fire. They all wanted to see the same film; in a few minutes they would turn on James Stewart. There would be no sense of peevishness about who sat where, about the position of honour nearer the fire or nearer the set. Nobody was hunting for a magnifying glass or a draught excluder.

Noel and Avril sighed.

'I'm sorry about the grannies!' Avril said suddenly.

'It would be nice if you could have normal Christmas Days like other children do,' said Noel.

Their three children looked at them in disbelief. This was the first time that an apology had ever been made. Usually they had been told how lucky they were to have two grannies and even luckier that these grannies came for Christmas Day.

They had never believed it, of course, but it was like crusts being good for you and fast food bad for you – they heard it and accepted it as something people said. It had been said for so long now, it was part of the scenery. Much easier to listen to and ignore than this new unease between their parents and this sudden revelation that grannies were not a Good Thing after all.

Ann and Mary and John didn't like it. It changed the natural order of things. They didn't want things changed. And certainly not at Christmas.

'It's your day too, you know,' Avril said.

'More yours than theirs, in fact.' Noel's face was eager to explain.

In the firelight his three children looked up at him. They were going to hear no explanation. No accusations about aunts and uncles who didn't do their fair share. No words like 'burden' and 'nuisance'. Not at Christmastime.

They had to speak quickly to prevent things that shouldn't be said being spoken.

'We thought that we could record *Star Trek VI*, and sort of give them an update on who they all are, you know – Kirk and Spock and Scotty,' said John.

'And Granny Byrne might be in one of her remembering-Dracula-and-Frankenstein moods,' Mary said hopefully.

Ann, who had grown up this Christmas and understood almost everything, suddenly said in a gentle voice:

'And there really couldn't be much room for them in any other inn or they would have gone there, so they're lucky this is the best inn in town.'

The Christmas Child

There was an old story that when Paddy Crosbie was recording *School Around the Corner* for the first time, he asked a
small boy to tell him a funny incident. The child took a deep
breath and said, 'It was Christmas Eve, and my sister came in
the door from England and said, I'm pregnant, and Da said,
Beautiful effing beautiful and we all laughed.'

Dot laughed more ruefully than others because as she used to
say to herself ... it was her story exactly.

It had been Christmas Eve when she had announced the
same news. Things had been different back then. Very different. Her father hadn't laughed at all. He didn't even manage
a smile during the chilly January wedding. It wasn't as if he'd
been an old man, but he'd had an old man's attitudes and
hardness of heart. But then those were different times, and the
town was small. And most of all he blamed himself, he felt
he hadn't been parent enough for Dot, that somehow he had
betrayed his promise to Dot's mother who had died long long
ago.

It was useless Dot trying to tell him that no amount of

mothers would have kept her out of Martin's arms and that she felt nothing but delight to be having his child.

Her father had turned his head away, holding up his hands. The situation was bad enough, must she now glory in her ways?

Dot used to look at pictures of her dead mother and wonder would the reaction have been the same. Might her mother have held her and consoled her, congratulated her even?

But it was foolish to be sentimental, it might as well have been the Middle Ages in a small country town. No doubt the calm eyes of this woman in the photo frame would not have been calm at such news. And anyway it had all turned out so well, a beautiful daughter, Dara, born in the springtime, a happy marriage for years and years. Well, twenty years. And that was more than most people had. It was more than her parents had.

It had seemed natural to go and live with her father again. Why should the two of them live in big empty houses with their memories?

Dara had been against it. It would mean an end to freedom, she had warned, her mother would grow old before her time caring for Grandfather. It wasn't what Father would have wanted, Mother to be entombed with an old man, an old man who had been so disapproving of her. There had been no point in Dot trying to cover up her father's long sense of grievance about the shotgun wedding. It was there in every sigh and headshake.

Dara begged her mother not to go back to her old home. 'He was so cold to you there when you told him about me. Don't go back now just because he's ancient and decrepit and can't manage any more.'

Dot smiled. Her father was a sprightly pensioner, anything less incapable she had found hard to imagine. And they wouldn't be on top of each other. Dot would move in down in the basement. She could give her piano lessons there easily, the pupils wouldn't even disturb her father, they could come in by a separate entrance.

'You think too much about him,' Dara had grumbled. 'Mark my words, it won't work out well.'

But it had worked very well, the years living with her father. He had a busy life, filled with committees and friends, and little outings.

Time passed peaceably. Dara moved in and out of their lives, bringing laughter and friends. But never just one friend. Never the man she was going to marry.

Dot longed to be a grandmother, she wished that her dark, handsome daughter would find a man she loved and start a family. Dara wasn't getting any younger, but Dot reminded herself that Dara knew only too well what age she was, she would scarcely appreciate her mother reminding her.

So Dot was always bright and interested in stories of new friends, new interests, new and bewildering successes at work. Dara, small dark eyes, Dara, the light of her life, was apparently a killer in the money market. She talked of stock exchanges in Tokyo and New York as easily as her mother and father had talked of music examinations for their pupils, as her grandfather talked of the Parish Council.

Dot sighed, they had wanted the best for their only daughter, she and Martin had travelled long hours on buses in the rain to teach in schools, they had taken the tone deaf children of ambitious parents and forced scales and tunes into them in hours of joyless work. There had never been a car, even when they could afford one, always keep a nest egg there, just in case. Dara might want to do a Masters in America, they would need the funds.

And they had never regretted a minute of it. Martin and Dot rejoiced over their daughter, and they forgave Dot's father his headshaking, his sense of lives destroyed, marriage anticipated and lingering shame. That was the way he was, it was his generation, they had told each other. The man remembered tales of the Easter Rising, before the founding of the State. How could he be expected to understand what was going on?

Always around Christmas time Dot felt glad that there had been no coolness, no falling out or even a sense of distance between them. She decorated the old house as she had done for as long as she could remember.

It was somehow unchanging. Dot would put on her wellingtons and go out to the walls in the long wet lane behind their garden, and pull great fronds of ivy. She ironed and folded the red ribbon each year so that it was ready to drape in big loose bows around the house. Even when Martin had been alive they used to bring a lot of their Christmas cards here to make the place look more festive. Dot looked back on it all, the Christmases when Martin had carved the turkey, twenty of them and the ones that went before and came after, they were all a long continuous line, same red ribbons, same kind of ivy. Just Dara's face changing, growing up, growing older even. Last year she had looked drawn and tired. But she had assured her mother that she was well and happy. Dot knew better than to pry, and was never tempted to offer advice. What could a middle-aged piano teacher offer in the way of counsel to a bright young star of the money market?

Dot's father had brought out a tired, neglected potted palm to be added to the decorations. It was far from lustrous, but he was fond of it.

'I thought we could use this.' He sounded a little diffident.

Still, he was his old self, sure in the rightness of everything he believed in, which included leaving plants in the dark.

'It's lovely, I'll put a ribbon around it,' Dot said. Carefully she sprinkled a dusting of Christmas glitter over it. It looked quite splendid, she thought happily. Maybe this is what she and Martin should have done with their lives, run a flower shop, created sparkling Christmas decorations rather than teach un-musical children to play the piano. She was smiling to herself at the thought and didn't hear the door open.

It was Dara, back from wherever she had been ... certainly another country ... maybe even another continent.

They sat in the firelight, companions and friends as well as mother and daughter. Dara told of the terrible rush to catch the plane, of the traffic, the crowds, the shops. At the mention of shops she leapt up and opened a parcel. It was a beautiful red silk jacket for her mother.

'I couldn't possibly ...' Dot was astounded. It was designer fashion, something for a younger woman, not for Dot.

But her daughter's eyes were shining, she said that when she saw it ... it reminded her of the scarlet ribbons and all the wonderful Christmases here at home.

Dot blinked the tears of gratitude out of her eyes, she tried on the jacket. She didn't look like a middle-aged woman, she looked terrific. She stared with amazement at her reflection in the mirror.

Behind her she saw Dara's face. It looked different somehow, perhaps that was just because it was a reflection. Dot turned around but she had been right, there was something different, Dara was going to tell her something.

'I have some very seasonal news,' she said.

Dot's heart missed a beat.

'What are you telling me?' she said, her face full of hope.

'What you told Grandfather in this very house a long time ago,' said Dara.

It was another era, the girl stood there proud and sure, happy that her Christmas news was welcome, that this baby would delight as she had done.

Dot folded her daughter in her arms, she stroked the dark hair, she cried with happiness.

'And tell me about him, when will we meet him. When will you get married?' Dara pulled away.

'Oh mother, I'm not getting married or anything,' Dara said.

'No, no.' Dot's voice was soothing, she didn't want to spoil the moment, the wonderful Christmas moment.

'It was never on the cards. I mean that wasn't part of what this is all about.'

'I see,' said Dot, who didn't see.

They sat together in the firelight, she held her daughter's hand as she had done during Christmas times long ago. She rejoiced that next year there would be another person here. A baby looking up and smiling at the lights and the ribbons.

She wouldn't ask now, about the man who had fathered this child, but was apparently never part of anything that this was about. She would hear eventually about why marriage had never been on the cards.

She must get the words and the tone right when she was telling her father about it. She must try to make him see what she couldn't see herself.

There was a tap on the door. Dara leapt to her feet.

'Grandfather!' She threw her arms around him as she had always done, 'I'm going to have a baby,' she cried.

'Well, well, well. Isn't that great news,' he said. 'We'll have to have a bottle of champagne for that, what Dot?'

Dot looked at them amazed. Where was the freezing out of all those years ago? Wait until he heard the rest of the story! Dot's heart was heavy that his unexpected first reaction would be bound to change.

'*I'm* not getting married or anything, Grandfather, *I'm* not ready to settle down … if you see what I mean.' She looked at him confident that he would understand the incomprehensible. But Dot's father seemed able to understand twenty times as much as he had understood all those years ago.

'I think that's very sensible of you, but then you were always a sensible young woman. Dot, did you say you were going to get us a drop of champagne to celebrate or are you going to stand there until Christmas is over with your mouth open and your eyes like saucers?'